THE NIGHT IN QUESTION

A BURKE AND BLADE MYSTERY THRILLER
BOOK 2

MICHAEL LISTER

ISBN: 978-1-947606-87-6

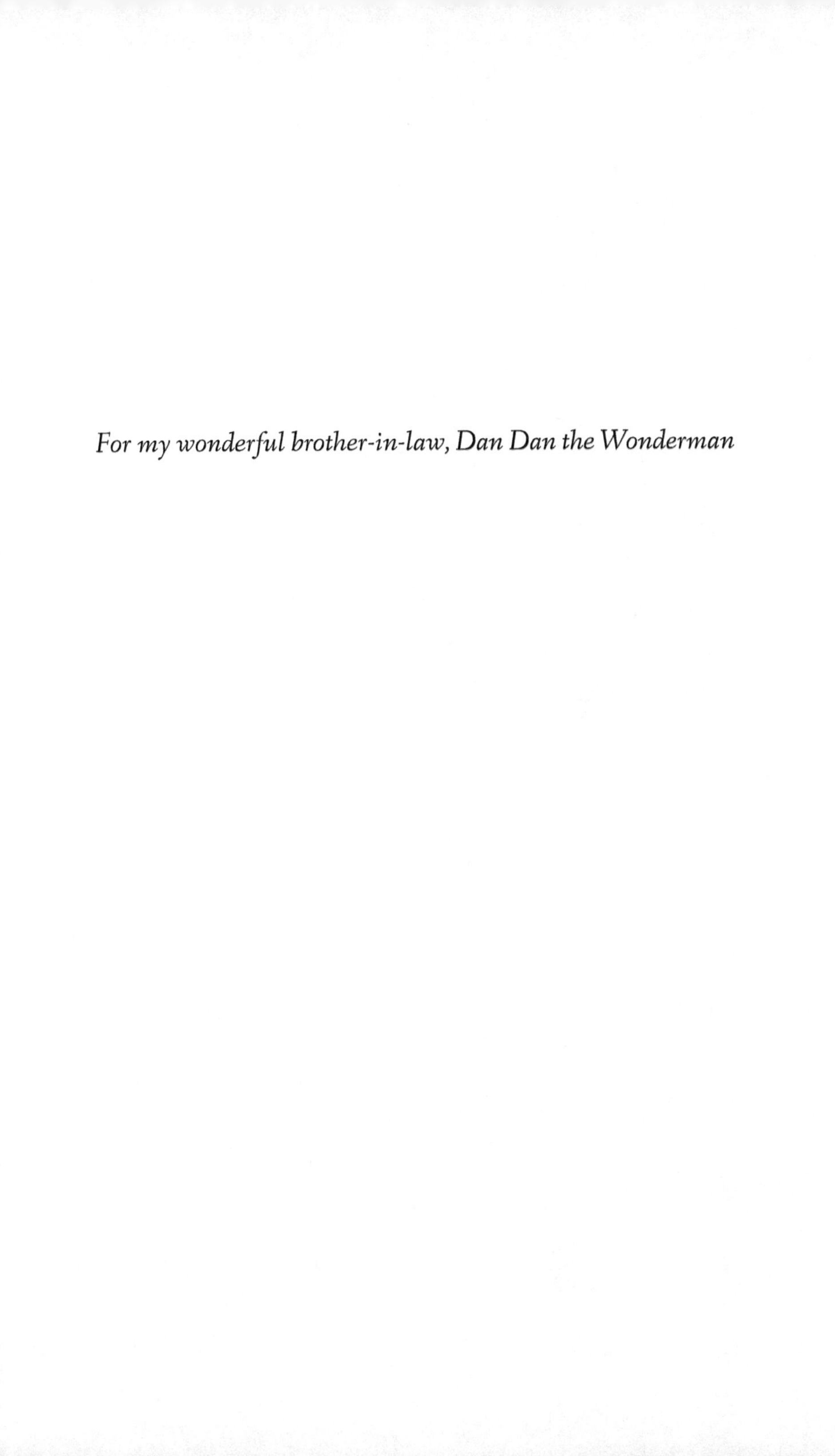

For my wonderful brother-in-law, Dan Dan the Wonderman

ACKNOWLEDGMENTS

Special thanks to Denise Lister, Jill Mueller Make Harrison, Rene Zemlock, Tim Flanagan for invaluable help with this book.

Cold Blood

Blood Betrayal

Blood Shot

Blood Ties

Blood Stone

Blood Trail

Bloodshed

Blue Blood

And the Sea Became Blood

The Blood-Dimmed Tide

Blood and Sand

Blood Lure

Blood Pathogen

Beneath a Blood-Red Sky

Out for Blood

What Child is This?

(Jimmy "Soldier" Riley Novels)

The Big Goodbye

The Big Beyond

The Big Hello

The Big Bout

The Big Blast

In a Spider's Web (short story)

The Big Book of Noir

(Merrick McKnight / Reggie Summers Novels)

Thunder Beach

A Certain Retribution

Blood Oath

Blood Shot

(Remington James Novels)

Double Exposure

(includes intro by Michael Connelly)

Separation Anxiety

Blood Shot

(Sam Michaels / Daniel Davis Novels)

Burnt Offerings

Blood Oath

Cold Blood

Blood Shot

(Love Stories)

Carrie's Gift

(Short Story Collections)

North Florida Noir

Florida Heat Wave

Delta Blues

Another Quiet Night in Desperation

(The Meaning Series)

<u>Meaning Every Moment</u>

<u>The Meaning of Life in Movies</u>

Sign up for Michael's newsletter by clicking <u>here</u> or go to www.MichaelLister.com and receive a free book.

ONE

"I'm about to die," Richard Iversen is saying.

He looks like he already has.

He's a gaunt, sixty-something, once white now gray man who looks a little like Nosferatu and smells like chemo.

He's seated between Malcolm and Heather Harrison across the desk from me in our office—a large room located inside the posh law firm of Lewinsky, Clemons, Bradley, and Sykes on 15th Street near St. Andrews. It had been decorated by a young, indulged female attorney from a family with money before she moved on to bigger and better things, leaving behind all her supplies and new furniture.

Our office is located here because we do some occasional investigative work for the firm, and one of the non-partner attorneys, Ben Simmons, is our foster brother.

Blade, my partner in crime fighting and sister in life, is hunched over the front right corner of the desk—half sitting, half leaning, one leg on the edge of the desk, the other on the floor. She resembles a slightly undersized collegiate linebacker. As usual, she is wearing a pair of black ninja webbing drop-crotch multi-strap cargo pants, matte black greasy leather boots, a black retro leather biker jacket with lots of silver-toned zippers and a buckle belt at the bottom, a plain black tee, and small round dark shades beneath a black snapback hat worn backwards. Every shade of black she's wearing either matches or compliments her dark eyes, hair, and skin.

We had formed an alliance as foster kids and been each other's person ever since.

"I'm trying to set my house in order and do some good before I go," Iversen continues. "This is something I should've done a long time ago. I'm ashamed that I didn't, but . . . I was overwhelmed by it all—not just the money, but losing my wife and all the publicity surrounding Leah's disappearance and . . . I kept thinking she would turn up."

Long before Richard Iversen was diagnosed with lung cancer, he had won a not insubstantial fortune playing the Florida Lottery.

Long before Richard Iversen won his windfall, his neighbors, the Harrisons, lost their little girl.

On a stormy night in October twenty-two years ago, Leah Harrison got out of her bed and snuck out of her house and went out into Tropical Storm Fernando—and vanished off the face of the earth.

Though not dying from an incurable and inoperable disease like their benefactor, the Harrisons look like people who have lived with the absolute agony of losing a child. They are extremely thin and pale, with dark circles beneath unfocussed eyes.

"Anyway . . . ." Iversen is saying. "I want to use all this money that I can't take with me to hire y'all to find Leah. To do what no one else has been able to do. Give Malcolm and Heather some answers . . . some peace . . . some closure. I understand that's what y'all specialize in—missing persons cases the cops have given up on."

"We do lots of different investigative and security work," Blade says, "but, yeah, missing persons cases . . . are sort of our thing."

"But," I add, "we've never worked on one where the person was missing for this long."

"Doesn't mean we can't," Blade says.

"I have plenty of money," Iversen says, "but I don't have much time. I want to buy results. I need you two to be honest with me. If I should hire a bigger firm, then tell me—and I'll give you a hell of a finder's fee just for telling me the truth."

"Burke won't say this," Blade says, "but I will. We're the best. You can hire a bigger firm, bring in some top guns from out of state and pay them a lot more money, but . . . you wouldn't get better results. No one knows this area like we do. No one has the contacts, the network. No one has gotten the results we have. And I'm not just talking about our famous cases like Amy Littleton and Nora Henri either, but all the ones that weren't splashed across the front page of the papers. And here's the thing . . . with your resources . . . if we need additional help, we'll hire it. We could even sub some of those bigger firms in Miami or Tampa or Atlanta if we needed to."

Iversen purses his lips and gives a slow raised-chin nod.

"What do you two think?" Iversen asks Malcolm and Heather.

"All we care about is finding out what happened to our daughter," Malcolm says. "We're overwhelmed that you're doing this for us."

"Should've done it a long time ago," Iversen says.

"We . . ." Heather says. "We'd never be able to accept something like this if it weren't for Leah. But it's still very difficult for us to accept. It's so . . . generous."

"It's just money and I don't have any use for it anymore."

"We're so very grateful you're doing this for us, Richard," Malcolm says. "And we'd spend all the money in the world to find Leah, but . . . but we don't want to see you just throw money away and not have anything to show for it."

Iversen nods. "Yes, as I said, I want to buy results and I want to buy them quickly. I'd like to be here when she's found."

Malcolm looks at me. "I'm not trying to be . . . But this is our daughter we're talkin' about here. She's all that matters. Finding her is all we care about. You mentioned not having worked on a case this old before. Haven't you been working on the Kaylee Walsh case a very long time and not gotten any results?"

Kaylee Walsh is our foster sister who went missing when she was twenty-one and we were kids. Her inexplicable vanishing is the reason we became investigators. When she was a junior at the University of Florida in Gainesville, for reasons no one has ever discovered, she lied to her professors about a family emergency and left campus without telling anyone. Later that night, on a flat stretch of rural road in Georgia, she ran off the highway into a ditch. Then, even with witnesses watching from a nearby farmhouse, in the span of some six minutes, she disappeared off the face of the earth without a trace. That was a decade ago, and Blade and I are the only ones still searching for her. The tenth anniversary of her disappearance is coming up and there was supposed to be a documentary made about her case, but it's now looking like it may not happen.

"*Malcolm,*" Heather says, her voice equal parts shock and reprimand.

"Oh, we've gotten results," Blade says. "Just not the ultimate result. Not yet. But we will."

"But," I say, "it does speak to the nature of this work. We

can't guarantee results. No one can. There's no case we'd like to solve more than Kaylee's. There's no case we'd like to solve faster than hers. So our lack of results is not the result of lack of effort. We can guarantee we'll work our asses off on your behalf, that we will use everything at our disposal—including our experience and expertise and the considerable network of contacts and connections we've built up over the years, but we can't guarantee that we'll be able to find Leah and we certainly can't guarantee we can do it quickly."

"We understand that," Heather says.

"All of that said," Blade says, "we your best bet at findin' your little girl."

TWO

"She wouldn't be a little girl anymore," Pete is saying. "She'd be close to thirty-two."

Pistol Pete Anderson is an investigator with the Bay County Sheriff's Office. He's a lean, clean-cut late-twenties white man with pale skin and short reddish-blond hair. And though his nickname has its origins in adolescence, he has become a world-class marksman winning regional, state, and national competitions—all in an attempt to change the narrative of his name. He's part of our network—a fellow survivor and foster brother of sorts and our primary law enforcement resource. It has become part of our routine to buy him breakfast and pump him for info at the start of each new case.

He swallows a big bite of eggs, grits, and bacon and adds, "She could have little girls of her own."

We are at Andy's Flour Power on Thomas Drive. Pete's having a more-than-full breakfast from both the Freshly Cracked Eggs and Friends with Benedict sections of the menu.

Blade nods. "Yeah, either we lookin' for a dead little girl or a live grown-ass woman."

"You know which the statistics say it is," he says.

"Yes, we do," I say.

"Everyone wants missing persons to be alive out there somewhere just waiting to be found," he says, "but that's never the case."

"Almost never," I say.

It's midmorning on a Tuesday between the breakfast and lunch rushes, and Andy's is busy but not slammed.

"So what's the deal with this case?" Blade asks.

Pete shrugs. "Dead ends, false leads, lack of evidence. Take your pick. It's probably the most infamous child abduction case in Bay County history, and the lack of results are not from a lack of effort. Twenty-two years later and we still have investigators working it. The original investigator is dead. He died a while back. It's easy to blame everything on him, but I don't think he did a bad job. Anyway, now we all take turns reviewing the file, following up new tips that come in."

"Still getting tips?" I ask.

"Nearly every week," he says.

"*Really?*" Blade asks, her voice rising in pitch and volume.

"It's a popular case—locally and internationally."

Blade's eyes spring open. "*Internationally?*"

He nods. "In the true crime community. There've been all kinds of podcasts and documentaries made about it. Got its own Reddit. Shit like that. Plus . . . the reward is up over a hundred thousand."

"*Whaaaa?*"

"It's been at forty-something for a while but then Mr. Florida Lotto kicked in another 60K, so now we're gettin' more than ever."

"So we solve this thing, we get a big fat bonus," she says.

Growing up in foster care and children's homes, Blade, like the rest of us, had never known financial security, and no matter how much we make or how big the balance of her bank account is, she never will.

"If y'all solve this one, you'll deserve it," Pete says.

"So, let's hear it," she says. "Take us through it. No time to waste. A nigga got some money to make."

Pete finishes chewing, takes a big swig of coffee, and says, "A ten-year-old little girl sneaks out of the condo her family is staying in during a tropical storm and is never seen again."

He starts eating again, and Blade shoots me an *Is he for real?* look.

"I could get more than that from the first line of the Wiki-pedia page," she says. "We didn't buy your ass two breakfasts for some shit my blind, deaf, and dumb grandmother could'a told us."

"Let me finish eating them and I'll go into more detail."

She turns to me. "He'll go into more detail once he's had his breakfast."

"And," Pete adds, "everybody knows your orphaned ass ain't got a grandmother—much less a Helen Keller one."

THREE

"On October 10, 2000, at sometime between midnight and two in the morning, ten-year-old Leah Harrison got up out of her bed, grabbed her backpack, and snuck out of the condo her family was living in, locking the door behind her."

Pete is telling us the story in a not un-podcast type manner from the back seat. We are in Blade's vehicle. I'm driving. We are headed to Flamingo South, the condominiums the Harrisons were living in the night Leah went missing.

The traffic on Thomas Drive is light and leisurely, primarily residents and snowbirds, with a few off-season tourists sprinkled in.

Planted palm trees in the median and on either side of the road remind us we're on vacation—or would be if we didn't live and work here. To our left, condos and townhomes are situated behind plaster and stucco walls and more shrubbery. Beyond them, mostly unseen, the bright white sands and clear green waters of the Gulf of Mexico. To our right, restaurants, bars, and shops that cater to tourists sit mostly empty on this weekday morning in October.

"Though everyone who knew her says she was deathly afraid of bad weather," Pete is saying, "she went out into a tropical storm. So far . . . no one knows why she did it or where she was headed—but it had to be something significant to her. The condo was small—two bedrooms. She shared a room with her younger stepbrother, Kyle. He heard her get up and just thought she was going to the bathroom. We don't know exactly what time it was, but her stepfather Malcolm had looked in on them a little before midnight and they were both there. Around two a storm chaser says he saw her walking east down Thomas Drive near the super clubs."

La Vela and Spinnaker were known as the super clubs because they were two of the largest night clubs in the world, and they were located next to each other right on the beach.

"A little later," he continues, "a trucker says he saw her headed west near the boardwalk. Both attempted to offer her a ride, but she ran away. The next day, some of her things were found in the storage unit of a townhome about halfway between the Flamingo and the super clubs. A full fourteen years later, her backpack was found buried inside two big black garbage bags some eight miles away in Panama City in the back lot of a church off Lisenby between 98th and 23rd. It contained several items—one of which we still have no explanation for."

"Like what?" I ask.

"It had some clothes, a book, some toys—no food or water or anything like that—and, strangest of all, it had a school picture of another little girl around her age who has never been identified. She wasn't a classmate of Leah's. She wasn't a student at any school in this area. And her picture has been posted everywhere for over twenty years now and . . . nothing."

"What was the book?" I ask.

"*The Secret Garden*," he says.

We pass Condom Knowledge, Splash Bar, Ms. Newby's,

Alvin's, and what's left of the super clubs, Le Vela and Spinnaker, which closed after damage sustained during Hurricane Michael and have yet to reopen. As I take in Thomas Drive, I try to remember what was here back in 2000 and what wasn't. The beach has certainly changed during that time, but many of the old landmarks remain.

Eventually, we arrive at Flamingo South near the west end of Thomas Drive, not far from the arcades and other tourist attractions on Front Beach.

Though it has undergone many facelifts over the years, Flamingo South isn't much to look at—a plain, painted-concrete behemoth of ten stories with a tacky pink Flamingo logo on the top center of the building. But it's not this basic boxy building but the beach beyond it that tourists flock to see.

We use the code Iversen gave us at the gate and pull in and park in the half-empty asphalt parking lot. He still lives in the penthouse suite, where he moved when he won the bulk of his money. At the time of Leah's disappearance, he lived in the unit next to theirs on the sixth floor.

"So," Pete says, "this is it. Not much to it, but . . ."

Blade looks up at the tall building. "So a ten-year-old little girl sneaks out of her unit on the sixth floor, takes the elevator or the stairs down, walks through this parking lot, gets past the locked gate, and makes her way down Thomas Drive in a tropical storm."

Pete nods.

"Tough little girl," she says.

He nods again, this time more enthusiastically. "They say she was rough and tumble. Bit of a tomboy. Hell of a basketball player for her age too."

"Still . . ." I say.

"Yeah," he says, "everyone says she was terrified of storms. Makes no sense that'd she'd go out in a storm like that. It was a severe one too. Right on the bubble between tropical storm and hurricane. Some people say it was up to hurricane strength when it hit."

"There must have been a hell of a strong motivation," I say. "We find out what it was . . . we'll be well on our way to figuring out what happened to her."

"The people living here at the time rarely locked their doors," he says. "Malcolm and Heather say they didn't lock their door that night, but it was locked the next morning, so . . . they believe Leah locked it behind her after she snuck out, as if to protect them or something."

"Malcolm is her stepfather?" I ask.

"Yeah. He had Kyle and Heather had Leah when they got together, but the kids were very young."

"What about Leah's bio dad?" I ask.

"He didn't do it," he says.

"How do you know?"

"He's dead," he says. "I mean he was even before this happened. Drunk driver T-boned his little Ford Contour at an intersection in Pensacola. He and Heather were never together really. They were very young. Went out a few times. She got pregnant."

We take the elevator up to the sixth floor. Even in October, it's damp and smells of chlorine.

When we step out onto the breezeway, a blast of wind blows in from the Gulf, the metal railing providing no barrier. It's a calm, clear day and this high up the gust is still powerful. I can't imagine what it would've been like that night.

We walk down the open breezeway, the Gulf to our left and to our right in the distance the kitschy and crass shapes of large wooden go-cart tracks, enormous plaster dinosaurs standing around green outdoor carpet putt-putt golf holes, and half of the sinking Titanic facade—most of which weren't here when Leah went missing.

We arrive at a small alcove with a door on the left and a door on the right—609 and 610, respectively.

"The Harrisons lived here at the time," Pete says nodding toward 610, and then jerking his head toward 609, adds, "and Iversen lived there."

He pulls out a key and opens the door to 610, and we follow him inside.

FOUR

The unit is small and looks like its primary purpose is as a rental. It's decorated, like most Florida condos I've seen, in bright, light colors—pastel beach and ocean scenes and faux nautical items. An anchor. A rudder. A wooden steering wheel.

A TV sits on a white wicker entertainment center in front of a couch and loveseat in a busy navy blue print with bright neon fish on it.

Tile floors throughout take away any sense of warmth, and cheap and worn furniture adds to the rental unit feel. There's also the hint of grit on everything from sand brought up from the beach on bare feet, flip-flops, and towels.

The entire unit is tiny, not much bigger than an efficiency apartment—four small rooms, a living room–kitchen combination, and two bedrooms, with a Jack and Jill bathroom between them.

In an attempt to make the cramped condo appear larger than it is, one entire wall of the living room–kitchen is mirrored.

"Oh, hello," Blade says to her reflection, then in her best

deep, demented Buffalo Bill voice, "I'd fuck me." Turning away from her reflection toward us, she adds, "Bet y'all thought that was Buffalo Bill from *The Silence of the Lambs*, but if you did, you'd be wrong. It was Jay imitating Buffalo Bill in the parking lot outside of Mooby's in *Clerks 2*."

"Masterful," I say. "The subtly and nuance of your performance was . . ."

"Lost on us," Pete says.

I look around at the cramped condo. "Small home for a family of four."

"Yeah," Pete says. "These units are made for vacationing, not living. Leah and Kyle had to share a room and all four of them were certainly on top of each other. But they didn't have a lot of options. Malcolm had lost his job and Heather was just getting back in the workplace after being a full-time mom. This unit belongs to Heather's rich Uncle Frank."

"I've always wanted a rich Uncle Frank," Blade says. "Or Sam or Ben or—hell, even a rich Uncle Buck."

"No way anybody named Uncle Buck could have money," I say. "You've got a rich Uncle Sam—he just wastes most of his money on his already wealthy nieces and nephews."

"Ain't that the truth," she says. "Be nice to have some rich relatives. *Shee-it.* Be nice to have some relatives."

"Yes it would," Pete and I say in unison.

"He still owns it," Pete says. "Don't think it gets much use. He's given us a key. Says we can come anytime we need to."

"Mighty white of him," Blade says.

We cross the small living room and step over to the small alcove with the three doors—bathroom in the middle and a bedroom on each side with less than a foot between them.

"That's the kids' bedroom on the left," Pete says.

"It's tiny," Blade says. "Kind of shit we used to have to stay in coming up—'cept there was usually more than two of us in there."

The sheetrock walls of the kids' room are painted seafoam green that clashes with the salmon bedspread and the blond-framed prints of purple porpoises.

The full bed nearly fills up the small room—leaving only space for a dresser and one bedside table. The single bedside table holds an eclectic stack of beach reads from true crime to romance.

"There wasn't room for two twin beds, so Leah and Kyle shared," Pete says. "Remember he thought she was getting up to go to the bathroom that night. I guess he fell back asleep and didn't realize she never came back to bed."

"Do you know if the parents' room door was closed?" I ask.

He shakes his head. "Probably in their statement. Not sure. Seems like it'd almost have to be for her to sneak out without being heard."

"You'd think a storm that bad and that loud would cause them to keep their doors open so they could hear the kids," I say. "And that they wouldn't be sleeping too soundly to begin with."

"My black ass wouldn't want to be up this high this close to the Gulf during a storm," Blade says.

"Here's the thing," Pete says. "They went to a hurricane party downstairs earlier that night, so . . . I think they were pretty well passed out."

"They'd have to be to sleep through the storm and their daughter sneaking out into it," I say.

"They feel guilty as hell about it," Pete says. "Blame themselves. But from every indication they were good parents, and they and Kyle have long since been cleared of any involvement. Interviews, alibis, polygraphs, and the DNA found on Leah's backpack and the things inside it."

"That's some serious clear right there," Blade says. "Like my teenage ass on Clearasil type clear."

"Your teenage ass couldn't afford any Clearasil," I say.

"Doesn't mean I didn't borrow some from the white-guilt foster families I cycled through, though, does it?"

"It's all in the file I've got for you," Pete says. "You can read it for yourself. I left it in the car. Remind me to give it to you when y'all drop me back off at Andy's."

The glass door of the balcony slides open, and we turn around to see Heather Harrison stepping into the condo.

FIVE

"I come here sometimes," Heather Harrison is saying. "To be near her . . . the last place I know for sure she was. And . . . in hopes that she'll come back here one day and find me waiting for her."

Heather and I are sitting on uncomfortable plastic band patio chairs on the balcony, the expansive green Gulf stretching out before us to touch the horizon.

A small low round table between us holds her journal, her phone, and a short stack of books—mostly poetry. I recognize one by Mary Oliver. There's also a paperback edition of Joan Didion's *The Year of Magical Thinking*, which I had read while I was inside.

Blade is running Pete back to his car and will come back here afterward.

"I know it's absurd," she says, "but . . . I can't help myself. We lived here for many years and every day I expected her to show up at the door. My uncle who owns it has been so good to keep it. If it weren't for my . . . fantasy or whim or whatever it is . . . he would've sold it a long time ago."

"I don't think it's absurd at all," I say.

She is so slight, so short and petite, as to be childlike. Her once flawless face has been etched by grief, and there's a paper-thin parchment quality to her skin. Still attractive, you can tell that she was once clock-stopping. Her primary allure now is rooted in sadness and a seeming certain indifference.

"Losing a child . . ." she says, then trails off.

The October day is crisp and clear, the midmorning sun high in the sky, its brilliance unmitigated by a single cloud.

"It makes you mad," she says eventually. "No other word for it. I know I'm damaged, my entire being off-kilter, but I also know there's nothing I can do about it. I suffer from an affliction for which there is no cure."

I'm not surprised by what she is saying, but I am by how she says it. I've spent a fair amount of time with a variety of broken people, many of whom were dealing with the loss of a loved one, and none of them were anywhere near this poetically expressive or possessed quite this vocabulary.

"Not that I want one," she adds. "I much prefer punishing myself every single second of every single day. Why did this happen? What actually happened? Who's responsible for this happening? Where is she? Will I ever know? What did I do wrong? How could I have prevented this from happening? These questions relentlessly torment me into madness and . . . I want them to."

I wait. I listen. I had intended to ask her several questions, but so far there has been no need for them.

"I wonder how many incidents in life cause one to look back and question every single choice prior to it," she says. "Not many I bet. But losing a child . . . a child who is still very much a child under your care . . . That'll certainly do it. I question everything—absolutely everything I've ever done. Every decision I ever made—including having children in the first place. Depending on what happened to her . . . it may have been far better if she had never been born. I feel guilty for thinking that, but then . . . I feel guilty for everything. But I feel most guilty for going to that lame hurricane party and drinking too much. But at the time . . . we thought . . . it's just a tropical storm . . . we're not going anywhere . . . no work the next morning . . . why not have a few cocktails?"

She pauses, letting the breeze take her words and swirl them about us before carrying them out over the Gulf.

"I can't forgive myself," she says. "Drinking to excess that night of all nights. It wasn't even something I ever did. I was never a big drinker. Haven't touched a drop since that night. Never will again. I can't. And I can't move on. Malcolm keeps telling me I've got to—or at least he used to. He doesn't tell me much of anything these days. I can't blame him. I actually can't believe we're still together. Can't believe a lot of things. Can't believe I'm even here. I'm an Air Force brat. My dad was transferred here my junior year of high school. Lived in many cool places before I wound up here in Podunk Panama City. Never thought I'd stay here, make a life here. I . . . was going to . . . see the world, have adventures, and write about them. I have a degree in English Literature and one in Creative Writing. Finished one right before Leah was born and got the other when the kids were very young. Planned on being a world-class poet before this happened. I still write a lot of poetry—probably more than I would have, but it's all about Leah and . . . loss, and no one's ever seen any of it."

As she speaks, she reaches over unconsciously and caresses the stack of books with her slight hand.

"Malcolm . . . Well, we're so different. I don't think he's read a single book since high school. Not sure he read any even back then. We're not just different people. We grieve very differently. For a long time he told me I had to let go . . . to do the whole Serenity Prayer—accept the things I cannot change. He's in AA. It saved his life. But . . . I can't let go. I can't accept this. He used to say I was still his wife and Kyle's mom and I had to be able to function in . . . those roles, but eventually he stopped. He could tell it was never going to happen."

Without seeming to be aware of what she is doing, she removes her hand from the stack of books and begins to touch and twist the small plain white gold wedding band on her finger.

"Something like this . . . It breaks everything. Malcolm has moved on—some, I guess. Certainly more than I have. In many ways we are strangers to one another. I'm genuinely and truly surprised each day when he doesn't come in and tell me he's leaving me. I guess he doesn't feel like he can. Doesn't matter. What would the point be? We . . . we share this loss—that's such a small and seemingly insignificant and inconsequential word for what we've experienced. But this reality-altering event binds us in a way that the wedding vows of impetuous young people never could."

As if just becoming aware of fingering her wedding ring, she abruptly stops.

"We aren't just broken. We're broke. We're poor and it's my fault. I don't contribute much of anything—a little money Uncle Frank gives me, but I can't work and haven't been able to since it happened. Not that a wannabe poet was ever gonna make much money anyway. And Malcolm . . . he's strictly a blue-collar worker. And he's too sad and broken and used to drink too much to be the kind of worker to get promoted or get a raise. I know it is an obvious remark, but what we're doing . . . it isn't living. We're not really alive but we're not completely dead either. We're like those poor souls who linger too long on life-support. I don't expect you to understand . . . and to be honest I don't care if you do. And . . . as much as I want you to find her for me, to . . . let me know what really happened . . . it won't make any difference . . . It won't unbreak us, won't bring us back to life somehow like Richard is hoping. Nothing can repair the rupture this has caused."

I nod very slowly and allow a moment to pass before saying anything.

Eventually, I say, "I understand."

"Well, you should also understand this—I'm not going to be any help to you. I don't remember anything from that night. I've tried. Believe me. I've tried and tried over the years. But I couldn't remember anything when it happened and I haven't been able to remember anything since. Except . . . there is one thing. I can't be certain. But I have this feeling I locked our door that night. We usually didn't, but with the storm and all . . . I don't know . . . Maybe I thought it'd help reinforce the door against the wind or something. Malcolm thinks we didn't lock it —or knows he didn't and thought it was strange that it was locked the next morning. Probably doesn't matter, but . . . Either way—whether it was locked or not—Leah would have to have a key to lock it when she left. It's just one of those things .. . I'm sure it doesn't matter. Except . . . I'm pretty sure Leah had lost her key."

SIX

"What're we doing here?" I ask as we pull into Pier Park.

While I was still talking to Heather Harrison, Blade had texted me to say she would wait for me in the car when she got back to Flamingo South so as not to interrupt any flow we might have found during the interview.

When I got into the car, she told me she wanted us to eat lunch at Tootsie's, which was just fine with me but I was shocked she wanted to.

Tootsie's Orchid Lounge is a bar and country music hall that began in Nashville back in 1960 when Hattie "Tootsie" Louis Tatum, a singer/comedienne with Big Jeff & The Radio Playboys, purchased a bar called Mom's and changed the name. The one located in Pier Park features some outstanding local and Nashville musicians.

Good music and good food is my idea of a good lunch, but it's not Blade's kind of place, and I'm curious why she wants to go there.

We park by the giant Sky Wheel, cross the street near the big beach ball in front of the Grand Movie Theater, and walk down the sidewalk, passing chain restaurants, souvenir shops, and distraction attractions like laser tag and ax throwing that cater to tourists.

"You still haven't told me why you want to go to Tootsie's for lunch," I say as we near the large purple storefront.

"Why wouldn't I?"

"Not your kind of place," I say. "Not your taste."

"Glad I can still surprise you."

When we step inside Tootsie's and I see who's playing, I have the answer to my question.

Cindi Rush, who usually plays with her band, Rush Street, is doing a solo acoustic set for the quiet afternoon lunch crowd. She's a young pixie with pink hair—a shaved undercut with a clean part, faded sides, and a soft quiff.

She's a good enough guitarist, but her money shot is her voice. It's soft, sultry, and sexy. She's playing a pink custom shop Taylor guitar that matches her hair, and the many earrings in her left ear wave about as she keeps the beat with her small head.

"This place might not run to my taste," Blade says, "but she sure as hell does."

"Are y'all seeing each other?"

"Not yet. Caught her with her band at House of Henri last weekend and been wantin' to break her down like a double-barreled shotgun ever since. Please tell me you know her."

Before I can answer, Rush says into the microphone, "Well, if it isn't my old friend Lucas Burke. How ya doin', man? I'll come see you on my break . . . and maybe you can join me for a song or two after you finish your BBQ sandwich."

"She even knows what you like to eat here," Blade says. "I've never loved you as much as I do at this moment."

We take a seat at a table to the left of the stage as Rush sings a slow, sexy version of "Losing My Religion."

"What did Heather say?" Blade asks.

"Nothing we didn't already know. That she's broken and nothing we can do—including finding out what happened to Leah—can unbreak her. She carries about as much guilt as anyone I've ever seen. She got wasted at the hurricane party that night and was passed out during everything. Doesn't even remember the elevator ride upstairs to their unit or falling into her bed."

We order, and when our food arrives Cindi's is with it, and she takes a break and joins us.

"Hey, man," she says to me. "So good to see you. It's been way too long. Where you been?"

"Spent a little stint inside."

"Oh shit. That sucks. Sorry to hear that, brah. Guess you still got that wicked temper of yours. You look good, though. Guess you survived it all right. You playin' any?"

"A few gigs in St. Andrews so far."

"We need to play together, man, you know? Get you back out there."

"Sounds good to me. You sound great. Rush, this is my sister Alix. Alix Baker meet Cindi Rush."

They shake hands.

"Everybody calls me Blade."

"Everybody calls me Rush. You were at House of Henri last weekend, weren't you?"

"Y'all've already met?" I ask.

"No," Rush says, "but she makes an impression."

"Wouldn't mind makin' some impressions on you," Blade says, her eyes locking onto Rush's.

"I don't think I'd mind that myself," Rush says. "But my girlfriend might."

"You ever find yourself freed up . . ." Blade says, "hit me up."

"I will. I definitely will."

The heat and intensity of the moment pass, and we begin to eat.

"I read about you two saving that little girl," Rush says. "You two are like internet famous crime fighters. Doing God's good work. Savin' children and shit."

Blade says, "Somethin' to keep in mind when you contemplating freeing yourself up or not."

Rush smiles and nods and her blue eyes twinkle beneath her pink hair. "If I had any real money, I'd hire y'all."

"Who you missin'?" Blade says.

"No one. They're missin' me, I guess. I'm bein' stalked. Harassed. Shit like that."

"Well, it just so happens we do pro-bono work," Blade says. "I'll be more than happy to help you out. Burke, why don't you go play a few tunes so she can break a little longer and tell me how I can—"

"Break her down like a double-barreled shotgun?" I offer.

So while Blade hears all about Rush's troubles and keeps the electricity of sexual tension arcing between them, I play "While My Guitar Gently Weeps," "Yesterday," and "Imagine" on a pretty pink guitar that doesn't match my light brown hair even a little.

SEVEN

Later that afternoon, after his shift has ended, we meet Malcolm Harrison on the Russell-Fields City Pier, the wooden pier that extends over fifteen hundred feet out into the Gulf of Mexico. The popular pier is located directly across from Pier Park, and we walk over after our late lunch with Rush.

As usual, the pier is busy—mostly with people fishing, but there are also a fair number of people enjoying the bright, clear day and hoping to catch a glimpse of a sea turtle or a stingray or a dolphin in the clear green waters of the Gulf below.

Malcolm's current job is as a cook at Margaritaville, and he smells of fried food and cigarette smoke.

He's trim and muscular, but his chef's uniform is baggy and loose. He's got thinning blond hair, sad green eyes, and an aura of tragedy.

"I still can't believe Richard is doing this," he is saying. "It's . . . He's always been a pretty selfish guy, you know. It's just . . . I guess it's what dying does to you. I don't know."

We are slowly making our way toward the end of the pier, the brisk Gulf breeze buffeting our already unhurried progress.

Along the way, we pass a variety of people fishing over the sides —including a double-amputee in the old-school wheelchair with the red bandana do-rag, aviator shades, and a tattered blue T-shirt with the white ADA wheelchair accessible symbol on it, the figure of a woman straddling the figure in the chair and the words "Wanna Ride?"

"I'd . . . sort of given up on us ever knowing anything," he says. "Not completely I guess, but . . . the police haven't done a whole lot in a long time—and really what is there for them to do . . . a case that old and all. I guess I thought the only way we'd ever know anything is if someone confessed. Some inmate in prison wanting to unburden his soul or something. I don't know. But I never expected this."

"This is the best chance in a long time to solve the case and find your daughter," I say. "We'll be applying pressure to everyone involved and that will cause things to happen."

He nods. "I hope it does."

"Never failed before," Blade says. "Shake shit up. Rattle some cages. Poke some bears. Exert some force. Take some actions . . . and get some opposite and equal reactions."

"I love my daughter with all my heart," he says. "I miss her every single day. Every single day. I want y'all to know that. I didn't let go of her. I let go of my attachment to the outcome, my . . . desire to control things I couldn't. And I did so not out of lack of love or care, but because I was caring too much—and about the wrong things—and it was driving me insane. I was drinkin' way, way too much. Drowning really. It's funny . . . Heather drank more than me the night of the . . . at the hurricane party and then never drank again. I started my real drinking in the weeks and months after Leah went missing. Took me years to get sober—or years before I was willing to even try to get sober. But I knew I had to. I knew that if we ever were going to find out what happened to her or even possibly get her back . . . I wouldn't be around for it. I . . . I don't care less just because I don't sit in that empty condo day after day wrapped up in some kind of quilt of guilt waiting for her to return."

I nod. "We know," I say. "We've done this long enough and experienced enough grief ourselves to know that everyone grieves differently and the way someone grieves is no indication of . . . anything, really."

We reach the end of the pier and stand next to the wooden railing.

"We know you love and miss your daughter," Blade says. "Help us find out what happened to her. What can you tell us about that night?"

He shakes his head and looks out at the Gulf. "Not much. I can tell you I should've never gone to that stupid hurricane party, should've never left the kids alone, should've never drank that much, should've never passed out when we got back home. We . . . we didn't even stay all that late. We were back before the storm really started. Stumbled in just as it was kicking off. I looked in on the kids as I lurched toward our bedroom. If I had been sober I would've stopped in and spent more time really checking on them. If I had . . . maybe none of this would've ever happened."

"But even in the state you were in," I say, "you could tell they were both there and okay."

He nods. "I . . . I used to be more sure about that than I am now, but . . . that's the drinking and the passage of time. It's been so long now. I can't remember anything. Not really. Not much. So . . . I have to go by my early statements. They are more accurate than my memory is, than my pickled brain is now."

"Were they awake?" I ask.

He shrugs. "I'm sorry. I'd have to go back and look at my

statement. I can't remember for sure now. I believe they were asleep. I'm pretty sure. They were in bed and very still. And . . . yes . . . I could hear their soft breathing. They were asleep."

"Did you see them again that night?" Blade asks.

He shakes his head. "I fell into bed and didn't get up again until late the next morning. I was so far gone . . . we both were . . . I can't believe I'm even telling you this, but we . . . We both pissed the bed and slept in it. Didn't even wake us up. My little girl . . . for some unknown and ungodly reason is . . . going out into that terrible storm and I'm . . . wettin' the bed and sleeping in it."

Tears fill his eyes, the wind coming in off the Gulf blowing teardrops onto the crow's feet at their corners.

We wait a few moments.

I turn and look back down the long pier at the invasive edifices encroaching on the coastline, the mammoth condos lining the beach as far as the eye can see in either direction, each enormous structure like the biblical houses built on sand looking like they could topple into the Gulf at any moment.

"When you *did* get up," I say, "and found her missing . . . What did you think?"

"At first I thought she was just somewhere in the condo," he says. "I was pulling the sheets off the bed when Heather came in and said she wasn't in our unit. I thought she must have gone out and down to one of the neighbors. We had told them not to ever go anywhere without asking, but I thought . . . she probably tried to ask and couldn't rouse us or did ask and we said it was okay but didn't remember. I can tell you what I didn't think —that something was wrong, that she was really gone, that she was missing."

"Who would she have gone to see?" Blade asks.

"Miss Barbara—a retired schoolteacher who always had cookies and loved for the kids to visit. The Scotts—a young couple who wanted kids but hadn't had any yet. Or her friend Sadie —a little girl near her age who lived there part-time with her dad. She alternated weeks between her divorced parents."

"What's his name?" Blade asks.

"Erik Arnold."

I make a mental note of each of these—though I suspect they're all in the file Pete gave us.

"What'd you do next?" she asks.

"We checked with each of them," he says. "And . . . to be honest . . . we were very . . . We didn't feel any sort of urgency or . . . We didn't think anything was wrong. We were very slow and casual about it. We had wicked hangovers and were moving like . . . We weren't moving fast, I can tell you that. Even after she wasn't at any of their places, we didn't panic, didn't think anything was wrong. We were more thinking about what her punishment was going to be for going out without telling us. The condo was big. The kids loved living there. They liked going to the pool and hot tub and the gym and the game room. We figured she was at one of those. After a while we checked all around the condo, and then when we didn't find her we began to get worried. Began calling everyone we knew. Enlisted our friends to help us look for her. Then eventually called the police and sank into the nightmare of her really being gone."

EIGHT

Later that night I keep Alana while her mom Ashlynn works her shift at Cloud Nine—a relatively new strip club in town.

Ashlynn is one of my foster sisters and a young single mom. Her four-year-old daughter Alana is smart, sweet, fun, and funny—and already striking with her dark hair and eyes and tan skin the color of polished sandalwood.

We are in my tiny apartment off Beck Avenue in St. Andrews playing a new game I got her—one in which you feed a toy pig purple, red, green, and yellow hamburgers until his clothes pop off.

My unit at Beach View Bungalows, which does not include a view of the beach, is small and only has three rooms—the main room, a bathroom, and a bedroom. As usual, it's clean and neat—apart from where Alana has strewn her toys about. As if living a spartan existence I didn't sign up for, there is very little furniture and few things in the place. The only thing of any value is an old Gibson acoustic guitar that a buddy of mine is letting me pay him for over time.

As we play, I attempt to read through the file Pete gave us, and even though I do it surreptitiously when it's her turn to roll the dice and feed the pig, she notices and will have none of it.

"Play with me," she says.

"I am," I say.

"Just play with me and don't do work."

Highly intelligent and keenly aware, not much gets past Alana.

"I have to do a little work tonight," I say, "but I'll wait until we finish our game, and you can watch a video while I do it. Okay?"

"Okay, fine," she says with all the weary exasperation and attitude of a teenager.

We play a few more rounds of Pig Popping or whatever it's called, and each time I work it so she wins, which she loves to do. Every time the clothes pop open and the pig's arms fly up, she squeals in delight.

As usual, I hug her a lot, expressing effusively just how much I adore her, how truly brilliant and fun and imaginative and beautiful I think she is. And as usual, she can only take so much of it before she shakes me off and tells me to stop talking and get back to playing.

I find my relationship with her fascinating. Though I'm a sort of father figure, we are also genuine friends. In some ways we are the best of buddies. I'm a single twenty-six-year-old male who is no blood relation, but we have been bonded since she was a baby and we've spent so much time together over the years that she feels like my own. She's not exactly an orphan like I was—or her mom was, but there's something about her being fatherless and her mom being so young working as a stripper that makes her in many ways seem like one to me.

"Luc, you miss when I'm not here, don't you?" she says.

I've told her so many times, and often as she's leaving I tell her I miss her already.

"Yes, I do."

And though it's true that I miss her when she's not around, my primary reason for telling her is how wanted and welcomed I want her to feel.

"I wish you would marry my mama," she says.

"She's my sister."

"I used to want to marry Sponge Bob," she says, "but now I want to marry Sonic."

"The hedgehog?" I ask.

"Uh huh."

"Cool."

I wish she wasn't already thinking about and talking about marriage at four, but I'm glad her choice in grooms runs to cartoon sea sponges and supersonic hedgehogs.

A little later, we are sitting together on the couch, snuggled up under a blanket, her watching *Sonic the Hedgehog* on my phone, me reading through Leah Harrison's file.

As I read, I can't help but think of how devastated I'd be if anything like this ever happened to Alana, and when I do, I can easily relate to the half-dead existence Heather Harrison is experiencing.

Reading the information Pete went over with us verbally this morning, I make a list of notes, questions, and to-dos.

1. What caused Leah to leave the condo and go out into the storm?

This to me seems the single biggest question and is foundational to everything else. If we can find or figure out what would motivate her to take such an extreme action, I think we'll be halfway to solving the case. In terms of motivation, hers has to fall within one of two broad categories—or both. She was either motivated by something inside the condo to make her want to leave or she was motivated by something outside of the condo to make her want to go out to it. Either way, the force of the push or pull had to be enormous for her to go out into such a severe storm.

2. Interviews we need to conduct: Kyle Harrison, Uncle Frank, Richard Iversen, Miss Barbara, Reginald and Valarie Scott, Sadie Arnold, Erik Arnold, the two witnesses who saw Leah out on Thomas Drive, the hurricane party hosts and attendees.

3. How closely were the tenants of Flamingo South looked at? Were there any sex offenders living there at the time? What about sex offenders living in the vicinity—especially in the direction she was headed.

After Alana falls asleep, I use my phone to search online to see what the true crime community has to say about the case.

There's the usual *the brother or the parents did it* theories—none of which offer any evidence at all and all of which ignore the evidence that exonerates them, including polygraph tests. There's the usual bizarre *alien abduction, she just ran away and is living somewhere happily,* and *child sex trafficking ring* theories. Again, with no evidence. Though everyone under the sun is listed as a suspect—including the Zodiac, the Atlanta Child Murderer, JonBenét Ramsey's killer, and Bigfoot. The name that is mentioned most is a sex offender living in the building at the time named Paul Darren Todd. But one of the most interesting and perhaps plausible theories is that at some point, Leah ventured too close to the Gulf and got sucked out to sea by the storm.

When Ashlynn arrives, her hair and clothes smelling of perfume, cologne, and cigarette smoke, her skin of heavily and sweetly scented body lotion, and her breath of booze, she is too keyed up to sleep, so we talk for a while—mostly about Alana, but eventually about our new case.

"He comes to the club sometimes," she says.

"Who?"

"The father. Malcolm. Saddest dude I've ever given a lap dance to."

"His wife is even worse," I say.

"I get it," she says.

"I do too."

We both glance at Alana but don't dare utter her name or anything about the possibility of anything ever happening to her.

"He's legit sad," she says. "You can tell. Some guys try all kind of shit to get over with you, you know? 'My wife won't fuck me. My wife died. I've got a terminal illness.' Shit like that. But his is real. All the girls feel sorry for him. Usually comp his dances and drinks and some of them let him feel them up a little. It's the saddest fuckin' shit ever. But it does seem to give him some kind of comfort. It's funny . . . I meant to mention the case to you and Blade a while back to see if y'all might help him, but I kept forgetting until I was back at the club and he came in again."

"He ever come in with anyone?"

She shakes her head. "Always alone. Sits at a table alone. And he never really initiates anything with the girls—except by tipping. He just sits there and sips his cocktail and looks at titties with those big sad, hound dog eyes."

"In my head I just heard Blade say, 'You know your ass is sad when not even titties can cheer you up.'"

She laughs. "I heard something similar. And it's true. It's totally true."

NINE

"Don't care how sad his ass is," Blade is saying, "wouldn't let him feel me up."

"Of course," I say. "But what if Cindi Rush was sad?"

"She could do all the feels. You right. Point taken."

We are in the parking lot of a large truck stop just off I-10 between Marianna and Tallahassee, waiting for the trucker who saw Leah the night she disappeared.

"You ever pity-fuck anybody?" she asks. "What am I sayin'? 'Course your sensitive ass has."

"You?"

"Nah."

"The more interesting question is has anyone ever pity-fucked us, and would we even know it if they did?"

"No way," she says. "Bitches be linin' up to get with this— the lipsticks and the butches."

I nod and smile. I believe that she's never been pity-fucked, but not for the reason she's saying, though that may be true too. She's never been vulnerable enough with any of her partners for them to have even considered she ever needed a pity-fuck.

"How about you?"

I think about it. "Probably. I can't think of any at the moment. One of the female guards in prison fucked me. It didn't seem like pity but it might have been."

"All this talk about fuckin' got me horny as hell," she says. "Shee-it. Wonder where Rush's fine ass is playin' today."

Dixie Lee Jennings pulls up and we get out.

He's a very thin man in his late fifties with a thick brown beard and long hair feathered in a flowing '70s style. From the shoulders up he looks a little like Kurt Russell in *The Thing* or *Escape from New York*, but only from the shoulders up. Because of his short torso and high waist, his long legs make up the bulk of his body. The top of his jeans and the enormous belt buckle hovering there seem to be right beneath his nipples, which show through the thin, silky button-down that, like his hairstyle, appears to be from the '70s.

His shirt is mostly unbuttoned, plunging down into a deep V that reveals thick gray chest hair and an early '80s-era gold rope chain.

"Like I said on the phone, I don't mind talkin' to you, but . . ."

We had spoken to him by phone, but seeing him now, I'm surprised we didn't have to contact him via CB radio.

"I can barely remember it all now," he continues. "There's nothin' I can add to what I said back then. When it happened."

"We understand that," I say, "but it helps us to hear it from you, and sometimes talkin' about it even after all this time will jar something loose."

"What were you doing out in that storm?" Blade asks, her voice inquisitive and interested instead of suspicious and accusatory.

"I covered a route for a buddy of mine whose girlfriend was havin' a baby. Took longer than I thought it would. At first I thought I could make it back before it got bad, and by the time it did I was stuck in it and I wanted to get home to my family. So I kept going. Just real slow. So it took a while. At the time, we lived in a little house off Rusty Gams and there was nowhere for me to park my rig, so I'd park it in one of the big parking lots of Spinnaker or La Vela and my wife or son would come pick me up. The storm was bad by the time I reached Thomas. I mean real bad. I hadn't seen a vehicle, let alone a person, for hours. I couldn't believe someone was out in that shit—and a little girl at that. Well, I thought I imagined it, was just seeing things. That can happen after driving so long and being so tired. Plus the wind and the rain had everything moving and dancing around, so I thought she wasn't there at first, but I kept looking. Rain was comin' down like a mother. Wind whipping everything around. Trees beaten to death. Power lines waving like jump ropes. Trash and debris bein' blown around everywhere. But I kept looking, straining to see, and I'm almost positive it was a little girl."

"Where was she?" I ask.

"Just on the side of the road, trying to make her way east but bein' blown about by the wind. I tried to pull up beside her and tell her to get in, but she darted down toward the beach. I've heard some people say that that's when she got . . . that by running away from me she ran too close to the water and got sucked out to sea. Hard to live with that. I hope to Christ that's not what happened. I was just trying to help. What the hell was she doin' out in that and why'd she run away from help?"

"What time was this?" I ask.

"Close to one, I'd guess."

"What was she wearing?" Blade asks.

He shakes his head. "Not sure exactly. It was so dark and it all happened so fast. Blue, I believe. A blue shirt or outfit or maybe even pajamas. I may have known back then—have y'all seen my statement? Did I say anything about what she was wearing then? I just have no idea now. I can barely picture her —let alone remember, if I ever knew, what she was wearing."

"Was she carrying anything or—"

"I don't know. I can't remember. We're talkin' twenty years ago. More."

"We appreciate you not just makin' shit up," Blade says.

"Yeah, I ain't gonna do that."

"Do you remember anything else?" I ask.

He looks up, squints, and purses his lips—all the deep lines on his face becoming even deeper.

"She . . ." he says. "She . . . I think maybe she moved funny. It could've just been the wind, but . . . I don't know . . . but it seemed like she was . . . hurt or injured or on something. I can't be sure—'specially after all this time—but something tells me something was wrong with her."

TEN

"Think she was wounded or—"

"Don't think he was so definitive in his original statement," I say. "Was he?"

We are back in the car, having just exited I-10 at Greensboro and headed to Torreya State Park.

"If she was hurt or whatever . . ."

"Could've just been the wind," I say, "but if it's not and he's right . . . the question becomes did she get hurt before she left? Is that why she left? Or did she get injured once she got out into the storm, which certainly seems like the most likely scenario."

"Probably just the wind and rain and his lack of visibility," she says.

"Could be that looking back knowing she went missing, his mind is projecting this onto his memory," I say. "Especially since he doesn't want to be responsible for her running toward the Gulf and getting swept out into the storm."

"True. And that's what could'a happened. Crashing wave knocks her down, undertow sucks her down, current sweeps her out. Months or years later she's the remains of a Jane Doe in Cuba or Mexico."

"We need to check unidentified female remains in her age range along every coast that borders the Gulf," I say. "Including the US states. And use DNA from her parents to rule them in or out. If that hasn't been done."

"Bet you a billion bucks it hasn't."

"Bet you're right."

"I can look into that while you're . . . in your meeting. See what's been done. What we can do if it hasn't. And prep for Kyle. 'Cause you know my black ass ain't about to take a walk in the woods."

My *meeting* is a clandestine assignation with my probation officer, Lexi Miller, in a yurt at Torreya State Park, after which Blade and I will be interviewing Leah's younger brother, Kyle.

"Thanks again for bein' willing to do this," I say.

"No sweat. Just be sure to let Rush know what a great gal I am."

"I absolutely will."

ELEVEN

Torreya State Park, named after an extremely rare species of Torreya tree that grows only on the bluffs along the Apalachicola River, was created by the Civilian Conservation Corps in the 1930s. It's a breathtakingly beautiful natural habitat for a dense forest of hardwoods and over one hundred species of birds. It is situated on a high plateau above the Apalachicola River with steep bluffs and deep ravines that plunge down to the river below and are covered with a wide variety of rare plants and animals.

But as rare and as beautiful as Torreya is, I'm not here to see it.

I've come to meet my probation officer and girlfriend, who because of the former is not allowed to be the latter.

We have to meet in secret and hide our budding relationship away from the rest of the world. And of all the places we've conducted our secret rendezvous, a yurt in a state park in the middle of nowhere has to be the most hidden.

A yurt is a portable, round tent usually covered with skins or felt and used as a dwelling by nomadic people in Central

Asia. The yurt in Torreya—the only one of its kind in the Florida State Park system, is a twenty-foot round domed tent with flooring and electricity. It has a lockable wooden door, three large, screened windows with flaps, accommodates up to five people, and, unlike the traditional yurts of Central Asia, is not portable.

When I arrive, Lexi is waiting for me inside.

She has just returned from a run and is stepping out of the shower when I walk in. Her blond hair, which touches the tops of her shoulders, is wet and has been combed straight back.

She is still drying off and I stand and admire her petite, athletic body.

When she turns and sees me, her Gulf-green eyes shimmer above her sexy little smile and she drops the towel and walks toward me.

We meet beneath the skylight and begin to kiss as she helps me out of my clothes.

When we're both naked and actively engaged in devouring one another, I turn and look for a place for us to land. The yurt is equipped with a full-size bed, twin bunk beds, and a queen-size bed.

"Have a preference?" I ask.

"I thought we'd use all three," she says. "So choose according to activity."

I do.

While lying on our backs on the second of the three during a rest and refractory period, we engage in whispered conversation.

"So cool of Blade to let us do this," she says.

"She's a good dude," I say. "And I've done the same for her."

"She's not just sitting in the car waiting, is she?"

"In the car, yes, just waiting, no. She's not the nature trails kind of girl, but she's not just sitting in the car on her phone—she's working."

"Of all the places we've met, this is my favorite," she says. "Feels safer. I feel more relaxed."

This is the farthest out of town and most secluded we've gone to so far.

"We should book it again," I say.

"And maybe stay overnight. In case they frown on yurt nooners."

"Definitely."

"We should plan a weekend away sometime soon too," she says.

"I'd have to clear it with my probation officer, but yeah."

I have anger issues. I sometimes explode. And my series of assaults and my many simple batteries and my general history of violence meant that when I was charged with aggravated battery for beating Logan Owens nearly to death, I was charged with a felony and sent to prison. Because my sentencing score sheet was so high, the judge sentenced me to a year and a day of state prison time, followed by two years of probation. If I ever violate my probation, I'll return to prison to serve my full sentence as well as any additional time I might pick up from the act that violated me back in the first place.

Lexi is a great probation officer and she takes an especially active role in my rehabilitation, making sure I'm not only meeting the conditions of my probation but truly working on dealing with my issues with rage and their underlying causes.

We're both taking an awful risk by seeing each other. If we are found out she will lose her job and I could lose my freedom.

Unfortunately, the worst possible person knows about us. Not only does Logan Owens, my supposed victim, know about us, but he has evidence—and not only of our relationship but of me violating the conditions of my probation. He holds it over me and has promised to blackmail me with it but so far has yet to ask me for a favor I can't refuse.

All of this is a weight on our relationship, a loaded gun pointed at us, which we try not to let in during our times together, but it's extremely difficult.

Getting away for a weekend and leaving all this behind us doesn't sound possible.

"Do you think she'd let you go?" Lexi asks.

"I feel like she would but won't know until I ask. I'd have to stay in the state, so we could go to St. Pete or Sarasota or St. Augustine—even Miami or the Keys, but if we did that, most of our weekend would be spent in the car."

"You still haven't heard anything from Owens?" she asks.

I shake my head and sigh. "Not yet but it's coming."

"Sorry. I said I wasn't going to mention it today, but . . . I couldn't help myself. Can we forget about him and everything else for a while and be the only two people on the planet?"

I'm doubtful we really can, but I nod and tell her we can.

As we begin to kiss and caress each other again, as we become each other's thresholds to the ecstasy beyond, I think of a line of poetry by Rumi and I whisper it as a kind of hopeful aspiration. "'Lovers find secret places inside this violent world where they make transactions with beauty.'"

TWELVE

There are approximately thirty degree-seeking theater students at Gulf Coast State College. Kyle Harrison, Leah's now twenty-nine-year-old brother, is one of them, but you'd never know it.

All the professors and students at GCSC know him as Hunter Harris.

"It's my stage name," he's saying. "But it's also a way to not be defined by one horrible thing that happened when I was seven."

Hunter Harris is thin with pale skin and thick, wavy black hair that stands several inches off his head. His boyish face is largely covered by a thick, black, and unruly beard he seems very proud of.

Blade and I are sitting with Hunter in the black box theater on the west end of the campus of the small community college that first opened in 1957 and is located at the foot of the Hathaway Bridge that separates Panama City from Panama City Beach.

One of only twenty-eight public colleges in the state,

GCSC has undergone several name changes, missions, and identities over the years—from Gulf Coast Community College to Gulf Coast Junior College and back to Gulf Coast Community College. Its most recent iteration happened in 2011 when it received accreditation to award four-year degrees.

"I don't mind talkin' to you," he says, "but I ask that you respect my privacy and identity and call me Hunter."

"Of course," I say.

"We ain't here to blow you cover," Blade says.

"It's not a cover."

She holds her hands up in a placating gesture. "Didn't mean anything by it. Just my way of sayin' your secret is safe with us."

"Sorry," he says. "I guess . . . I'm a little sensitive about it. I feel bad, but . . ."

"We understand," I say. "We really do."

The nondescript space we're in is dim and quiet. A single theatrical light hanging on a grid provides all the illumination—and does so in dramatic fashion—and the acoustics are such that there's a hushed, airy quality that absorbs our words almost as soon as they pass through our lips.

Small for a theater but large for a classroom, the high-ceilinged space we're sitting in is square and black with a flat, open floor. We're on portable, padded theater seats in the front row of a four-tier riser that holds about fifty of them.

The black box theater is a simple, flexible performance space with an understated and unadorned design. Made popular in the 1960s, they were inspired by the practice spaces of major theater companies and university drama programs.

Because it can be adapted to fit the staging and seating requirements of many different types of theatrical productions, the black box is used for small, intimate plays, experimental theater, standup, workshops, classics with little technical requirements, and everything in between—all of which allow for an acting-focused experience where the limited audience is mere feet from the performers.

"Anyway," Hunter is saying, "I'm not gonna be much help to you. I was so young and I just don't remember much. I was asleep for most of it."

"Well, we appreciate you talkin' to us," I say. "It really helps. I'd like to start with the days leading up to Leah's disappearance. How did she seem?"

He shrugs. "Like normal I guess. I was so young at the time and . . . you know, sort of self-involved I guess."

"Do you remember anything out of the ordinary happening?"

He looks up toward the single theatrical light in the far right corner and rubs his beard.

Eventually, he shakes his head. "No, not really."

"No?" Blade asks. "Or not really?"

"Can I give that one some more thought and get back with you?" he asks. "I feel like there might be something, but . . . I can't come up with anything specifically."

"Sure," I say. "You think of anything at any time—no matter how small or insignificant it seems to be—you let us know, okay?"

He nods.

"What kind of relationship did you and Leah have?" I ask.

He shrugs again. "I would've said typical brother and sister but the more I see of other siblings . . . I'd say we had an above average one. And it was because of Leah. The older one . . . sort of . . . I don't know, dictates the . . . way you relate, I guess. She was very sweet to me. Very patient and . . . I don't know, included me in stuff. She was fun. Always had somethin' goin'. Some kind of adventure. Some kind of game or playacting thing. Pretending with her is probably why I'm a theater major. It's funny . . . I never thought about it before like that."

"How about your folks?" I ask. "How'd y'all get along with them and how did they get along with each other?"

"Back then . . . before . . . *it* happened . . . they were pretty cool. They weren't after. Not even close. Not ever again. But before it . . . I don't know, broke them . . . they were chill and kind of fun . . . sort of groovy, I guess."

"What did y'all do while they went to the hurricane party?"

"Mostly played. I can't really . . . I remember we kept looking out at the weather to see what it was doing."

"Were y'all scared?"

"Anxious, I'd say. She must have been because I feel like I usually just mirrored how she was feeling."

"How often were y'all there alone?" I ask.

He shakes his head. "Can't ever remember another time when we were."

He runs his hand through his thick, puffy hair and gives his head a little shake to tousle it into place.

"I feel so bad," he says. "I wish I could've . . . prevented what happened. Wish I could remember more now. But I was a kid, you know? Just . . . kind of into my own thing. I feel guilty about changing my name too, but . . . you can't imagine the shit I've been accused of. People are vicious. Especially online. Not many people know what Burke Ramsey feels like, but I do. It's . . . You have this horrific experience of losing your sister, which is the worst thing imaginable, but then . . . it actually gets worse because people accuse you of the most horrible things—saying I killed her, and . . . The reasons they give for me doing that are . . . I can't even begin to . . . How sick do you have to be to accuse a seven-year-old of the rape and murder of his ten-year-old sister? And this was well after the police had cleared me. The detective working the case and the child psychiatrist both said I didn't do it, but these trolls aren't about to let a little thing like that stand in the way of them coming up with the most bizarre theories and outrageous scenarios. I realize I'm hiding, but . . . I don't know what else to do. I'm a mess, but nothing like my poor parents. I guess I was young enough for it not to fuck me up quite as much as them."

"Again, I'm so sorry for . . . all of it—your loss and then all you've been subjected to since then. I know you've got class in a few minutes. Could I just ask you a few more questions and then maybe we can pick this up again another time?"

He nods. "Can't be late to class. Already have been too many times."

"Did Leah have any friends your parents didn't know about?"

His eyes narrow and his brow furrows. "Can I think about that one and get back to you? I feel like she might have."

"Did she talk to, call, or write to anyone during that time that—"

"I think she had a pen pal," he says. "It's just so hard to remember. I'll look through some old things when I can and see if I can find anything or at least jog my memory."

"That would be great, thanks," I say. "Did she get hurt or injured in any way that night?"

"Not that I can—wait. She got hurt playing basketball. Not that night but a few days before. Think she twisted her ankle or something. Which is like this whole other layer, you know? Like why would a little girl who's afraid of the dark and storms and who has a bad ankle go out into that?"

"Can you think of any reasons why?" I ask.

He shakes his head. "I've tried. Broke my brain straining to come up with something, but . . . never have."

"Did anything happen that would make her want to leave the condo that night?" I ask. "Anything at all?"

"No," he says. "Nothing. The only thing that was . . . anything at all was the storm, and that would've made her stay in."

THIRTEEN

I'm sitting at the end of the counter in the St. Andrews Slice House reading Marcus Aurelius and eating a slice of Thai-Pocalypse when Clyde Broussard walks in.

Pizza is my favorite food and the Slice House is my favorite place to get it. It's a small joint just off Beck with the best crust and truly unique toppings—and it happens to be a very short walk from my apartment.

It's late on a school night and the place isn't as packed as it usually is. I have the end of the counter to myself.

Clyde Broussard is an enormous black man with both a big belly and plenty of muscle. Everything about him is thick, including his hands, which resemble old, weathered catcher's mitts. He has to turn his wide body to angle through the back door.

When he takes a stool beside me, my pulse quickens and my anxiety spikes.

Clyde is Logan Owens's bodyguard and enforcer.

Logan Owens is the reason I went to prison. Without any irony at all, our fucked-up legal system considers him my victim, and because one of the conditions of my probation is to have no contact with him, Clyde serves as the go-between.

"Burke," he says.

He's looking with bemusement at the homemade videos of stunts gone wrong showing on the monitor mounted to the wall.

"Clyde."

"Good book?"

I nod.

"Better than watching bitches break they balls, I bet," he says.

Because he can't know that the stool can shoulder all his weight, he keeps his feet on the floor and keeps a certain percentage of the load on them.

"I've never eaten here," he says. "It good?"

"The best."

"What's that you got there?"

I tell him.

"Holiday in Cambodia" by the Dead Kennedys is playing loudly on the little house system, and no one can hear our conversation.

"What all's on it?"

"Oil, garlic, mozzarella, curry chicken, yellow onion, and sweet Thai chili sauce."

"Damn," he says. "Gonna have to try me some of that sometime."

"You should."

"I been tryin' to see you for a while," he says. "But you've always got that stripper's kid with you and . . ."

"I really appreciate you waiting until she's not around."

"I do things a certain way. Show respect. Don't fuck with women and children."

"Your employer does," I say.

"Hasn't while I been around," he says. "Won't while I'm around."

"Then I'm glad you're around."

"I'm here 'cause Mr. Owens got a job for you," he says.

I knew this day was coming. Logan Owens has video footage of me committing battery on one of his employees. The man had threatened to rape Lexi and loosed my rage on him. He didn't fight back because the entire thing was a setup created for the purpose of blackmailing me. Now I have to do little jobs for him or he'll turn over the footage to the DA and I'll go back to prison.

Clyde says, "Here's the thing. He's not gonna ask you to do anything illegal and he's not gonna do anything illegal with anything you produce. You have my word on that. This is not a good situation, but let's see if we can't make the best of it. Like I said . . . I do things a certain way. Same as you. We sometimes work for people who don't have our same . . . rules, but we make it work. Let's see if we can't make this work."

"What's the job?"

"It's a straightforward simple one. Mr. Owens been seein' this little honey that works over at Cloud Nine with your girl. He wants to make sure she's not steppin' out on him—not seein' anyone else, not makin' extra money on the side sellin' her sweet little ass. That's it."

"So what happens to her if I find out she is turnin' tricks?"

"Nothin'. He'll break it off."

"More likely he'll break something off inside of her," I say. "He's not just gonna walk away. He's a sick, vicious prick who likes to hurt the vulnerable. And what is this girl, eighteen but looks thirteen? You and I both know he's not into grown women."

"I have convinced him it's in his best interest to protect his business and stay out of prison and to do that he's got to stay inside certain . . . parameters."

"Even if you have and even if he is legit tryin' to do that, eventually he's going to revert back to his factory default settings and do real damage to someone who can't protect themselves."

"That's what I'm for," he says. "I'll protect them. I'll protect him from himself and them from him."

"I don't doubt you'll try," I say, "but . . . you can't be with him twenty-four-seven. Where is he now? And who's with him?"

"I've got it covered. It's not just down to me."

Though I can't help but feel like I'm Roy Horn of Siegfried and Roy putting my head in Montecore the tiger's mouth, I say, "What's her name?"

FOURTEEN

"So now we workin' for the little weasel," Blade says.

"No," I say. "Not *We. I.* It's not an agency case. *I* am. I don't feel like I have a choice."

It's the next morning and we are speeding across the state on I-10 toward Lake City to meet Ethan Storm, the storm chaser who saw Leah on the night she vanished.

"Fuck the agency," she says. "That's just a name and you know it. Everything is *we*. Everything. You know that. There is no *I* in any of this shit, and you know it."

Behind us is a blue sky with quilted clouds beyond which is a big, bright seemingly close sun. Before us, in the distance, a bank of battleship-gray clouds gather and with them a descending darkness.

"So *we* are working Rush's stalker?" I ask.

"I know if I need your help all I have to do is ask."

"Of course, but—"

"But what?"

"This whole Logan Owens thing isn't even a case. It's a mess I made. It's . . . my fault. I don't expect you to—"

"Help you clean up your mess?"

"Yeah."

"Bitch, I'm your ride or die and you know it."

"I just feel guilty since it's my— It's a problem I created."

"You know good and goddamn well I would've done the same shit you did," she says. "The only things I'm concerned with now is keeping you out of prison and takin' that prick down. You got a plan for any of that?"

"Not a plan exactly, but . . . I'm gonna go along with this girlfriend investigation thing to try to stall and buy time. I'll do whatever I can to keep him on the hook until I figure out something—or, and this is what I'm really hoping happens, he gets arrested or is taken out by . . . one of his associates."

"Me and Pete workin' on bringing him down," she says. "Buyin' time ain't a bad strategy. Clock's gonna run out on that twisted bitch eventually."

"Meantime I'm gonna keep an eye on the girl."

"So it's not one case but two we just picked up?" she says. "We gonna investigate the girlfriend for Owens *and* we gonna protect *her* from *him*."

"Yeah."

"And figure out what happened to Leah Harrison and find Kaylee."

"Yeah."

"And on the weekends stamp out rightwing domestic terrorism and bring peace to the Middle East."

"Somebody needs to."

We fall silent a beat, each of us taking sips of our convenience store coffee from the brightly branded Styrofoam cups it's in.

"Still not sure it's worth the drive just to talk to Storm in person," she says, turning back to the task at hand.

"Probably not," I say, "but no way to know. And I always like looking in their eyes and observing their body language."

Ethan Storm is heading down I-75 toward an Atlantic coast storm and has agreed to meet us for a few minutes where I-10 and I-75 intersect near Lake City.

"You think that's his real name?" I ask.

"Not a chance," she says.

"But if you're gonna change it," I say, "why not change it to Stormchaser?"

"You know what they say about him," she says. "If he shows up in your town, it's time to get the fuck out of Dodge."

"Yeah."

"And yet we drivin' toward him."

We meet Ethan Storm at an enormous Busy Bee truck stop that has more people, energy, and activity than some small towns I've seen.

As we park and get out, Blade says, "Still wish we'd've met at Café Risqué instead."

Café Risqué, the infamous 24-hour truck stop/restaurant/titty bar, is only about another hour down 75 from where we are now.

"Me too, but he picked the place, so whatcha gonna do? Besides . . . this place has a Dunkin."

"Man, fuck donuts when you can have titties."

The Busy Bee is like a convenience store and a rest stop on steroids—rows and rows of snacks and chips and candy, aisles and aisles of touristy buy-out-of-boredom bullshit, massive coolers with every brand of soda, a huge wall of fountain drinks, an enormous deli, and in the back, both a Burger King and a Dunkin Donuts.

We find Storm standing near the rows of wooden barrels filled with candy. He has the rugged look of a storm chaser— dark complexion, sun-lined face, unkempt hair, scraggly beard

—all except his size. He's a petite little dude of about 5'4". As if the result of a head stuck on the wrong body, he has the face of a badass adventurer and the body of a boy.

He's wearing a bright blue short-sleeved nylon Bahama-style Columbia shirt with mesh-lined vents in the back and four chest pockets in the front, a pair of knee-length drawstring khaki shorts, a pair of ankle-high waterproof leather work boots, and a pair of Maui Jim shades dangling from the retainer strap around his neck.

I can see why the camera loves him—and it's not just his angular face and sharp jawline, but his wide-eyed openness and the bright-toothed quick-flashing smile.

"I appreciate you meeting me here," he says. "Gives my crew a chance to snack and fuel up."

"We appreciate you being willing to talk to us," I say.

"I just don't want to have wasted your trip, but I'm afraid I have."

"Especially since we don't get to see no titties," Blade says.

He smiles. "My guys wanted to meet at Café Risqué too but I didn't know if y'all'd be into it. And it would've meant driving another hour for y'all."

"We'll drive almost any distance for titties," Blade says.

"Good to know if we ever meet again. 'Course the farther south you go, the worse the weather's gonna get."

"Speaking of that," I say. "How bad was it the night you saw Leah?"

"Nothin' like Michael that pummeled y'all a few years back, but it was bad."

Hurricane Michael was a Cat 5 superstorm that struck our region over three years ago—one we still haven't recovered from.

"It was supposed to be a tropical storm, but it intensified in the final few hours before it came on land and it was a hurricane," he says. "I shouldn't've been out in it when I was—and I was in a big SUV designed for storm coverage. I couldn't believe a little girl was out in it. I thought . . . I thought I was seeing things at first. You do sometimes. Especially in storms like that one where everything is moving, being blown around —and it's late at night."

"What time was it?"

He shrugs. "I can't remember a lot of the details, so I don't know exactly, but sometime between two and four in the morning."

Blade says, "And you sure it wasn't just . . . an optical illusion or some shit like that?"

"Like I said, I thought it was at first, thought it had to be, but I did a double and triple take, then I turned around and tried to go help her. I definitely saw her."

"Where were you and where was she when you saw her?" I ask.

"I was coming down Front Beach," he says. "Took a right on Thomas . . . and saw her pretty soon after that. She was walking down the side of the road. I'd say somewhere between Pineapple Willy's and the intersection of Thomas and Front Beach."

Though closer to Flamingo South, this is in the opposite direction from where Dixie Lee Jennings saw her.

"Which direction was she headed?" I ask.

"Toward Front Beach."

So not only was she in the opposite direction but she was heading farther that way.

"You sure?" Blade asks.

He nods. "Positive. There's plenty I'm not sure about, but I know where and when I saw her."

"Was there anything odd about her movements?" I ask. "Did she walk like she was injured or—"

He shakes his head. "Nothing like that."

"What happened when you turned around to go offer her help?" I ask.

"As I was turning, my headlights moved across her for a moment, but by the time I got to where she had been she was gone. I searched for her for a few minutes, but never saw her again."

"Any idea where she went?"

"No, but . . . I could see the road and the sidewalks and the fronts of the buildings, so she had to have gone behind the buildings on the beach side. Nowhere else she could've gone—unless she went into one of the buildings, which is what I thought must have happened that night."

"Do you remember what she was wearing?" I ask.

"Not really," he says. "Not with any certainty. Like a yellow rain slicker over a blue outfit maybe."

"And you're sure it was her?"

He nods. "When I saw the picture of her and heard what happened, I knew for sure."

"Did you think something different before that?"

"No, not really. Obviously, I didn't know who she was or the circumstances, so . . . Before I knew who she was . . . I wouldn't've thought she was that young. I thought she was older, but I never could've imagined a ten-year-old out in a storm in the middle of the night like that."

FIFTEEN

"So the trucker says he saw her down by Le Vela and little storm chaser man says he saw her near Front Beach," Blade says. "Can they both be right or is one of them lying?"

"Or mistaken," I say.

We are back in the car, headed west toward home and the blue skies on the horizon.

"Or mistaken," she says.

"We need to figure that out," I say. "Can you pull the file out? 'Cause they don't just see her in different places but they describe her in different ways. If they both saw her, then we know more about her movements, but if they didn't, then we need to know which one really did."

She pulls the file off the back seat and begins flipping through it.

"Dixie Lee says he saw her down by the super clubs, right?" I say. "But what time? And what did he say she was wearing?"

"He said it was between twelve-thirty and one and she was wearing a blue outfit—maybe pajamas. No mention of a yellow raincoat."

"We need to go walk it to see if it's even possible for her to have gotten to the spot where he says he saw her by the time he says he saw her, and then see if she could've gotten back to the spot where Ethan says he saw her by the time he says he saw her."

"You can walk it," she says. "I'll follow you in the car and time it."

I laugh. "*Thanks*," I say. "But I don't want you to overexert yourself. If they both saw her, then at some point she puts on a yellow rain slicker over her blue outfit. Why not start with it if she had it, and if she didn't, where did she get it?"

"Neither of them mentioned a backpack," she says.

"I thought Dixie did."

"Nope. Not in his original statement."

"Interesting. Okay, so we've got to walk it and go over their statements again and compare them with each other, but . . . let's say it's at least possible."

"It's at least possible," she says slowly. "I thought we were saying that together."

"Think about Leah getting up out of bed and going out into the storm," I say. "We keep sayin' there had to be a powerful motivation for her to do that, right? Especially as scared of the dark and bad weather as she was. So this whole time I've been thinking she had some place she felt like she had to go."

"Yeah?"

"Like somewhere specific," I say. "But if both witnesses saw her, then she didn't go to a specific place. She didn't even go in a specific direction. She went in two different directions."

"She's a young kid. Maybe she got lost, turned around in all that wind and shit."

"True."

"But . . .?" she says.

"But?"

"I just felt a *but* coming."

I shake my head. "Not a but exactly. More of a . . . Just a thought. If they both saw her and their times are right, then that means she went east on Thomas Drive, then at some point later turned around and went back west."

"Yeah?"

"Think about where Ethan says he saw her."

"Yeah?"

"She would've had to walk back past Flamingo South," I say. "She would've had a chance to go back inside. Get out of the rain and wind. Dry off. Get back in bed. But instead she continued past it in the other direction."

"You right," she says. "Whatever she was doin' . . . she was committed to it. Couple of hours out in all that shit didn't make her change her mind—even when she came back so close to her home and could'a just gone in."

SIXTEEN

When we get back to town, we drive straight out to Flamingo South.

Blade drops me off at the gate.

I start the stopwatch on my phone and begin moving slowly down Thomas Drive.

I'm about six feet tall and have a much larger stride than Leah, so I take small steps and move as if there's strong wind and rain buffeting my progress.

I walk east toward the super clubs where Dixie Lee Jennings says he saw Leah the night in question.

Thomas Drive is four lanes, but the speed limit is thirty-five. Off-season traffic is light and slow. Walking is easy along the planted palm-lined sidewalk, and even at my slow pace, I make good progress past the condos, townhomes, and the enormous site of the Boardwalk Beach Hotel and Convention Center. At the intersection of South Thomas Drive and Thomas Drive, I hang a right at the KOA Campground, walk past Category 5 Cafe and Ms. Bubba's Pizza, and over to the entrances of the now dilapidated super clubs of Spinnaker and La Vela.

After a few moments, I press Stop on the phone's stopwatch and take a screenshot of the time. I then press Reset and Start and head back the way I just came. Only this time, instead of stopping at Flamingo South, I continue on past Pineapple Willie's and Laketown Warf Resort, and up to the traffic light at the congested intersection of South Thomas and Front Beach.

After waiting a few moments, I again press Stop and snap a screenshot. I then walk back over to Laketown Warf, where Blade is waiting for me.

Laketown Warf Condominiums is a massive multi-story condo with five pools, a putting green, a large freshwater lake with a light-up fountain show, and several shops and restaurants.

I meet her at Juan Taco, the small, modern boutique taco shop.

I find her at a table in the back reading over the file.

"Well?" she asks when I sit down across from her.

I nod. "I think she could've done it."

"Both?"

"Yeah. I walked very slowly and—"

A young woman with dark hair held back in a ponytail wearing a Juan Love T-shirt with the multi-colored and groovy-patterned hand symbol for *I love you* walks up and places our food on the table—beef tacos and sangria for me and quesadillas and a margarita for her.

"Thank you," I say to her.

"Let me know if y'all need anything else," she says, and walks away.

"And thank you," I say to Blade.

"Thank Richard Iversen, not me," she says.

"Thank you for ordering it and having it ready when I got here."

"So . . . you walked very slowly and . . ."

"Really took my time and waited extra time once I got to each sighting spot. If she left the condo around midnight, she could've made it to Le Vela and Spinnaker between twelve-thirty and one and back here at the intersection with Front Beach by two. And that's factoring in stopping at the storage unit she visited and little side treks. Doesn't prove she was at both places when they said she was, but it's at least possible."

"I've reread Dixie Lee's and Ethan's original statements," she says. "They're a little more detailed than what they remember now, but nothing they told us contradicts what they told the cops back then. Dixie Lee says he saw her close to Spinnaker and La Vela around one, that she was wearing blue —maybe pajamas—and that she moved like she was injured. Ethan says he saw her close to Front Beach between two and four and that she had a yellow rain slicker on, but maybe some blue clothes beneath it. Neither mention a backpack. We now know it's possible they both could'a seen her."

"If they did . . ." I say. "Why did she change directions? Was she not headed somewhere in particular? Did something scare her or was debris blocking the road? Did she get confused, turned around? Where did she get the raincoat? Why didn't she have it on from the beginning? We know she stopped in at the storage unit at the townhome when she was headed east on Thomas. That seems the most likely place to have picked up the raincoat."

"Owner don't say nothin' 'bout a raincoat goin' missin' in her initial statement."

"Maybe she didn't realize it had," I say. "Let's go ask her."

SEVENTEEN

The Sandpiper is a set of townhomes located near the west end of Thomas Drive in a small section of single-family homes and townhomes—the few remaining Davids in between the Goliaths of high-rise condos and beachside businesses.

Marjorie Whitten-Collins is an elderly woman who has to be in her late seventies, though she doesn't look it. She's an old-school hippie and activist with wealth and power—at least at the local level. She's thin with long gray hair and a dark tan. She's dressed stylishly and expensively in a kind of Boho chic islandy Danika dress with ethnic-inspired environmentally aware accessories. She looks like a well-traveled, intelligent, and inspired gypsy—who was willing to pay a lot to achieve that particular look.

"Not many people we're talking to still live in the same place twenty-two years later," I say.

She is walking us around to the storage units at the back of her townhome.

One block from the beach, the townhome is surrounded by

a tall, black metal-framed dark wood privacy fence that makes the space feel like a compound.

"We wouldn't be here if the developers had their way, but they haven't been able to price me out yet. And I don't plan on letting them. This is a good place to keep an eye on them and good a place as any to die in."

"*We?*" Blade asks.

"Well, I'm not sure how I meant it," she says. "I guess I meant it two ways. On the micro level—me and my son who lives here with me. On the macro level—all the homeowners in the area who refuse to sell. Anyway . . . the poor dear broke into my storage unit back here that night and stayed for a while. It's this one."

The small structure housing the four storage units is located on the side of the property at an angle. Each of the four single doors has a number on it that corresponds to the number of the townhome it belongs to.

She unlocks and opens the door and we look inside.

About the size of a prison cell, the small, unfinished space is filled mostly with plastic storage crates and cardboard boxes. Hooks screwed into the unpainted particle board hold everything from yard tools to a bright blue kayak.

"I wish she'd've stayed all night. I wish I would have discovered her here the next morning so I could've offered her breakfast, a warm bath, dry clothes, and helped her with whatever she was dealing with."

"Wonder what made her stop in here." I say. "And what made her leave again. It's not that far from where she started."

"I wish I knew," she says.

"And how could she even get back here?" I ask.

"We've always assumed she either climbed the fence or the storm blew open one of the doors. There are three doors—two for pedestrians, one in the front, and one in the back, and a wide gate for vehicles."

"Were any of them open the next morning?" I ask.

She shrugs. "I'm sorry, I just can't remember. But it has happened several times over the years—especially in severe weather. Latches don't hold."

"Was the storage unit locked?" I ask. "Did she actually have to break in?"

"It was only locked about half of the time," she says. "It's pretty safe back here. The fence keeps most people out. And there's nothing of value in it anyway. I'd be happy to give anything to anyone in need. But it must have been unlocked that night . . . because there was no sign of forced entry."

"Did you hear or see anything that night?" I ask. "Anything at all?"

She shakes her head. "The storm was so loud. I mean, I heard a lot of noises but thought they were all storm related."

"Who all was here that night?" I ask. "We'd like to speak to your son or anyone else who was here."

"Ah . . . he's not home right now," she says, stumbling over her words for the first time. "I can set up a time for you to talk to him, but he . . . He's . . . He won't be much help. He has a brain injury."

"Sorry to hear that," I say. "But . . . if it's . . . If it wouldn't be too . . . We'd still like to talk to him at some point if that would be okay."

"No problem. We'll figure out the best way to do it and get back to you with a good time."

"Thank you. I really appreciate that. And we won't be . . . We'll make it quick and as painless as possible. Do you remember what she left and what she took?" I ask.

"She left some candy wrappers, a soda bottle, a hair clip, a school pencil, a little Giga Pet, and a few other random small toys."

"A Gigawhatta?" Blade says.

"A Giga Pet," she says. "It was a digital pet kids took care of —had to feed it and care for it, raise it from egg to adult. It came in a little plastic candy swirl shell about the size of a small egg with little buttons on it and had a hole at the top so you could put a chain through it and wear it like a necklace. They were very popular back then. All the kids were wearing them and raising them and trading them."

"Do you remember what was in here at the time?" I ask.

"Not really," she says. "Probably about the same as now. Mostly seasonal decorations, some old clothes, a few folding chairs, a tent, our beach stuff."

"Did she take anything?" I ask.

"I don't think so."

"What about a raincoat?" I say.

"I . . . I'm just not sure. I don't think so."

"Would there have been one in here at the time?" Blade asks.

"It's entirely possible," she says, "but I probably couldn't've told you back then and I certainly have no idea now."

EIGHTEEN

"You get the feelin' she don't want us talkin' to her kid?" Blade says.

We are back in the car driving toward town.

"That exact feeling," I say.

"We gonna need to follow up with him, 'cause I doubt we'll be hearin' from them."

"Wonder what Pete knows about him," I say, pulling my phone out of my pocket and calling him.

He doesn't answer and a moment later I get a text from him that says he'll call me back as soon as he can.

"I know I keep sayin' it," Blade says, "but keep in mind how far this is."

We're driving from the last location Leah was seen alive to the place in town where her backpack was discovered so many years later.

At the east end of Thomas Drive just past the naval base, we take a right onto 98 and cross over the Hathaway Bridge.

Continuing on past the college and the port, we cross over

Beck at St. Andrews and when we finally reach Lisenby take a left. About a mile and half down Lisenby we take a right into Horsley Construction Group across the street from Greenwood cemetery.

Parking in front of the large gray building, we get out and look around.

"This used to be a church," I say. "Unity of Panama City. It was built in 2001, so when Leah went missing . . . it was probably just a vacant lot. I'm not even sure if it had been cleared or if construction had begun."

"We don't know that her backpack was buried back then," Blade says. "Could'a gone into the ground much later."

"True," I say. "All we know for sure is that in 2014 as a member of the church was cleaning or clearing in the back of the building, he unearthed a large black garbage bag and in it another big black garbage bag and in it Leah's backpack."

"So sometime between October 10, 2000, and—do you remember when it was dug up?"

"August 16, 2014."

"So sometime between October 10, 2000, and August 16, 2014, the backpack Leah left with the night she vanished was buried way over here—nearly ten miles from where she went missing."

"So bizarre," I say. "Why bury it here? Why bury it at all?"

"You wrap it in two plastic garbage bags, you plan on preserving it so you can come back to it," Blade says.

"Did you read about this in the file?" I ask. "It says they brought in ground-penetrating radar and cadaver dogs to search for Leah's remains but found nothing."

"Do we know if anyone connected to the case has any connections to this property or the church that was built on it?"

"I've never seen anything about that, but we should look into it."

"They say the ground-penetrating radar didn't find her remains in the ground," she says, "but what if they're in the foundation? Would they show up there?"

"We need to find out," I say. "What're you thinkin'? Someone abducts her and keeps her for a while and then buries her here when they're doing construction?"

"Something like that, yeah."

"Why don't they bury the backpack with her?"

She shrugs.

I say, "I guess if they did that, they wouldn't be able to come back and get it or visit it."

"Makes sense—I mean like serial killer sense."

"But if her backpack and the things in it are trophies for her killer, why not just keep them? Why bury them? And why here?"

"Good questions."

My phone rings and I look at the screen. It's Pete.

"You callin' to tell me y'all've solved the case?" he says.

"Just got two quick questions," I say.

"Shoot," he says.

"Did y'all interview Arthur Whitten-Collins? File doesn't mention him."

"I believe they did, but I'll have to—hold on a minute."

He puts me on hold.

When he comes back, he says, "Yeah. They did. Sweet guy. Brain injury. Didn't know anything."

"How thorough was the search for Leah's remains where her backpack was found?"

"Extremely," he says. "It was all thorough. The church was very cooperative. We used dogs and GPR. She's not there."

"Not even in the foundation?"

"Not even in the foundation. Nowhere. Just the backpack. Strange, isn't it?"

"Yeah. Anyone connected to the case also connected to this property or the church?"

"That's three questions, but I'll allow it. And the answer is —not that we ever found."

NINETEEN

That night I have a gig at Little Village.

Little Village is a shopping and entertainment venue located on Lake Ware in St. Andrews, specializing in live music, island food, and fair-trade gifts from around the world.

I'm set up beneath the palapa, the huge, open-sided thatched roof covering out back, the setting sun streaming in refracting off every reflective surface and the smooth waters of the lake behind me.

I've had Alana since I got home, and it was a challenge to get ready and get her ready and get her here and set up and do a soundcheck while caring for and entertaining her.

By the time I start my first set, I'm pretty tired and a little frazzled, but it doesn't take long for the music to calm and soothe me.

I open with Neil Young's "Harvest Moon" and go straight into Peter Frampton's "Baby I Love Your Ways."

It's just me and my guitar—my favorite way to play these days—and I lean into the mellow acoustic vibe. The small crowd visiting and eating fish and shrimp tacos seems to appreciate the soft, slow groove.

While I'm playing, Staci, Alana's dad's mother, is watching her at one of the tables. Though her son is not involved in Alana's life, she occasionally is, though usually for very short periods of time. An hour or two at a time seems to be her limit. My gig is three forty-five-minute sets with two fifteen-minute breaks, and the fact that Alana already looks restless and Staci isn't doing anything to entertain her doesn't bode well for me getting to finish it.

This adds another layer of stress because I really like playing here and don't want to lose this gig.

When I finish my next song, Jason Isbell's "If We Were Vampires," Alana runs up with a crumpled dollar and drops it in my tip jar.

"Thank you, sweet girl," I say.

"Luc, are you almost done?" she asks, her tone full of boredom and impatience.

"Not yet," I say. "Hang out with your grandmother and have fun. I'll be done in a little while."

"Can I stay up here with you?"

"Go back with her and I'll come see you in just a minute."

"I want to play with you," she says, her voice rising.

I can feel a tantrum coming on, and as much as I don't want to give in to it, I can't deal with it right now and I know Staci will be no help.

"Do you want to play a song with me?"

"Okay."

I pull out a small tambourine and hand it to her.

"You stand right over here and play with me, okay?"

When she turns around and sees the audience watching her, she gets shy and shrinks in a little on herself, but she takes her job seriously and when I start playing she joins in.

I try to think of something simple with a good steady beat that she might like and settle on "Peaceful Easy Feeling."

She stays on the beat better than I thought she would and for the moment the crisis is averted.

As we are playing, Lexi walks in with a group of her friends.

When Alana sees her, she drops her tambourine and runs to her, squealing her name as she does. "Miss Lexi!"

Lexi picks her up and hugs her and acts genuinely happy to see her, and when she and her friends take a table, Alana joins them.

I play another few songs and then break a little early. "I'm gonna take a short break," I say, "then I'll be back for two more sets. Thanks for hanging out with me tonight."

I rush over to Lexi's table, say hi, and attempt to get Alana to come with me.

"No, I want to stay with Miss Lexi," she says.

"Your grandma is missing you," I say, though when I glance over at Staci she's on her phone, oblivious to Alana or anything going on over here. "And I need you to help with more songs."

"No. I want to stay with Miss Lexi."

"Let her stay," one of the women says. "She's so cute."

"We'll be on our best behavior," another one says.

Lexi nods and says, "It's okay. Really. She can hang out with us."

The other friend, a slightly older woman with too much makeup, jewelry, perfume, and self-tanner, leans in and says, "And how do you two know each other?" Her voice is full of innuendo and undertone.

Lexi eyes widen as anxiety ripples across her face.

I pause for the slightest of moments trying to think of how to respond.

"Work," I say.

"Quit being so nosy, Deidre," Lexi says, her voice playful on the surface but with real bite beneath.

"It was nice to meet you ladies. Thanks for letting Alana—"

"Work?" she says. "That's kinda vague. And is this y'all's love child?"

"This is my little buddy, Alana," I say. "She's my niece. I keep her while her mom's at work."

"And what kind of work does your mom do?" Deidra asks Alana.

I cringe, my viscera clenching in dread as I await her response.

"She's . . . She works in the cloud," Alana says.

"Like on the web or something?"

"*Yes*," Lexi and I both say.

"Stop with the interrogation," Lexi adds, "and let Luc get back to work."

"Well, if you'd ever tell us anything I wouldn't have to be so—"

"Let me know if there's anything y'all want to hear," I say. "And I'll come back and get her in a few minutes. Thanks again and it was nice to meet you."

"It was very nice to meet you, handsome," Deidra says, and like most of what she says it sounds flirtatious and sexual.

I open my second set with the Avett Brothers' "No Hard Feelings" and then play a string of Beatles, Dylan, the Stones, the Mamas & the Papas, Cat Stevens, and Jim Croce, combining some of them into medleys and mashups along the way.

While I'm in the middle of "Let it Be," Staci gets up, clears her table, grabs her purse, and leaves, pausing briefly to say something to Lexi and Alana on her way out.

By the time I finish my second set and take a break, Lexi's

friends have gone and she and Alana are coloring in a tattered-cover coloring book.

"Sorry," I say. "What did Staci say?"

"Just that Alana looked happy with us and that she had to go."

I shake my head. "Unbelievable. Are your friends gone? Sorry about that too. I hope that didn't embarrass you too bad. Did they ask you anything else?"

"Deidra did, of course. All of them said how handsome and talented and nice you were and where had I been hiding you and why hadn't I married you yet."

"Nothing else about how we know each other?"

"Not really. A little from Deidra. She won't stop until I give her a satisfactory answer."

"I'm so sorry."

"I chose to bring them here," she says. "It's my own fault for wanting to show you off, even though I know I can't. Anyway .. . I'm happy to stay and watch Alana or I can take her back to your place so she doesn't have to sit here for another hour."

"I wanna go play," Alana starts singing. "I wanna go play. I wanna go play."

"You sure?" I ask.

She nods. "Absolutely. Happy to do it."

"I'll hurry home as quickly as I can, as soon as I get done and—"

"Why don't you swing by Cloud Nine when you finish here and see if you can talk to Logan Owens's latest victim. What's her name?"

"Destiny. Are you sure?"

"When else are you gonna do it? We'll be fine. I'll text you if there's a problem, but there won't be. She's already eaten. I'll play with her and bathe her and put her down. And who knows

. . ." Her voice drops. "If she's sleeping soundly when you get in, maybe you and I'll play a little too."

TWENTY

I'm sitting at a small round table by myself near the right side of the main stage in Cloud Nine.

It's still early—a little before ten—and the crowd is relatively small.

Ashlynn is dancing on the second stage, and I'm looking everywhere but over there.

The two stages of Cloud Nine are rectangular with a pole on each end and are located out in the middle of the floor so patrons can stand on all sides.

As usual, it's loud and cold and smells of body lotion, booze, and cigarette smoke.

Winston is working the door and Declan is in the back at the entrance to the VIP section. Both men are enormous with plenty of both fat and muscle, their masses barely being held back by their 5XL white shirts and black vests.

The monotonous, incessant house music is dance versions of popular songs with a constant mechanical pounding of the floor on the four beat. I can't imagine having to hear this all night every night, and though everyone who works here makes good money, they're not making enough.

Destiny Diamonds is on the main stage, working both the pole and the customers gathered around the stage.

Because I want to talk to her, I grab my stack of singles and approach the stage.

At the three-minute mark of "Pour Some Sugar on Me" by Def Leppard, the DJ fades it down and brings up AC/DC's "You Shook Me All Night Long."

No matter the actual length of a song, the DJ fades each and every one at the three-minute mark because the customers getting lap dances in the back room pay per song.

Standing at the stage, I wait my turn, and when she finishes being tipped by the other men here to admire her, she makes her way over to me.

She's a tall, thin, leggy platinum blonde with plenty of long hair extensions, huge fake boobs, and a flawless airbrush spray tan.

Even before she starts her routine, I begin showering her with singles, using an excessive amount to get her attention.

"Big spender, aren't we, baby?" she says.

Wearing only a T-back G-string and eight-inch clear acrylic platform heels, she gets on all fours in front of me, her feet hanging over the edge of the stage, and wiggles her little ass. She then turns around and lies on her back and lifts and spreads her legs. As she shakes her feet in the air, I shower her with even more singles. Winking at me, she caresses the narrow patch of cloth above her crotch. For her finale she gets on her knees and places her plastic boobs in my face.

Everything she does has a robotic feel to it and she, like every other stripper, does the same things for every tipping customer. How any guy can convince himself that it's personal or that she's actually into him is astounding and says more about our species than I wish it did.

When I give her the rest of my singles, she leans into my ear and gives me a lip-trilling purr, then whispers, "Thank you, baby. I'll be over to see you in a minute."

I return to my table and wait.

The dancers don't make their money on the stage—even when they are well tipped by a big crowd. Their real money is made back in the VIP room from private dances. After a dancer does her three-song stint on the stage, she goes around and thanks all the men who tipped her, typically sitting with the customer who tipped her the most and attempting to sell him on a trip to VIP.

I watch as Destiny flitters around from man to man, touching and thanking each of them, until she lights on me.

"How are you tonight, baby?" she asks, taking a seat beside me.

"I'm good. How are you?"

I try to come across as naive, wide-eyed, and a little slow.

"Good, yeah," she says as she looks around and signals for one of the cocktail waitresses.

"Buy a thirsty girl a drink?" she says when the waitress reaches our table.

"Of course," I say. "Anything you like."

"I'll take a Red Bull and vodka," she says.

"I'll have the same."

"Thank you, honey," she says as the waitress hurries off to the bar.

"My pleasure," I say. "You been dancing here long? I haven't seen you before."

"Not too long. Just needed some extra cash to pay for my college classes. I'm going back to school to be a nurse. I like helping people."

"If I ever woke up in the hospital and saw you, I'd think I had died and gone to heaven."

She smiles. "Speaking of heaven . . ." she says, glancing and nodding toward the VIP entrance in the back. "It's right back there if you want to go."

"Oh, I'd love to. You would do that with me?"

"Sure, sugar."

"How much is it?"

"You can't put a price on paradise, baby, but it's ten for the room for half an hour and twenty plus tip per song."

Apparently, you *can* put a price on paradise.

"I would love that. Can we have our drinks and get to know each other a little first?"

"Absolutely, baby."

The unseen DJ fades "Bad Girlfriend" by Theory of a Deadman and brings up "I Luv Dem Strippers" by 2 Chainz with Nicki Minaj.

The waitress returns with our weak drinks on her little round tray, overcharges the shit out of me, and gives me my change back in singles.

When I tip her and she leaves, Destiny says, "Tell me about yourself."

"Me? Well, I'm a lawyer—"

"A lawyer? You don't look like a lawyer. You any good?"

"Haven't lost a case yet. What do I look like?"

She shrugs. "A musician, maybe, or like a beach bum. You look like you get up to no-good . . . a lot."

"How about you?" I ask. "Tell me about yourself. Any kids? Husband? Boyfriend? What do you like to do?"

"No kids. No boyfriend. Just little 'ol me. I like going to the beach. I like shopping. I love to cook."

We sip our drinks and look around the club—at the other strippers working the other patrons just like Destiny is working me. I try to avoid looking at Ashlynn, who is now at a table with a college-looking kid across the room.

"We can take our drinks with us to VIP," she says. "I just can't wait any longer to be alone with you."

"Sure, okay," I say, and hand her the money for the room.

I hadn't planned to take her into VIP, but the thought of doing so with someone who Logan Owens cares enough about to hire me to check up on is irresistible. He ruined my life and is now blackmailing me. The least I can do is have his girlfriend rub her nearly naked body on me.

When she returns from paying for and booking the room at the front desk, she picks up her drink, takes my hand, and says, "Let's go have some fun."

She then leads me through the club to the VIP entrance in the back.

VIP at Cloud Nine is a dim hallway with small rooms off to one side, each more like a booth than a room and with a curtain instead of a door.

Declan smiles and nods at me as we pass him. "Room seven," he says. "You two kids enjoy yourselves."

"He a friend of yours?" she asks as she leads me past the other curtained booths to the last one on the left.

I nod.

"He gave you the most private room in the place. We can do whatever we want."

Inside the small, mirrored booth, she sits me down on the built-in cushioned seat and starts undressing.

When she has stripped down to only her T-back G-string, she moves me to the center of the seat and straddles me.

"You're so handsome," she whispers in my ear, "and I'm so horny. You're not like the other guys who come in here."

When the next song starts, she begins to move around on me, purring in my ear and placing her breasts in my face.

"Kiss me," she says. "Touch me."

Out of habit, I have my hands down at my sides. Technically, the customer is not supposed to touch the dancers.

I know enough to be able to report back to Clyde who can in turn tell Logan that surprise surprise, his stripper girlfriend is actually just giving him the girlfriend experience, but suddenly I don't want to stop. And it has nothing to do with Destiny, who I don't find attractive. It's all about doing things to Logan's girl.

I put my mouth on her nipple that is closest to me and my hands on her body—first her hips and then her breasts.

I feel bad for Destiny, or whatever her name is. I feel guilty and ashamed—especially because though Lexi and I haven't defined our relationship, we are in one of some kind. I feel sleazy and a bit morally bankrupt. But I can't stop. I don't want to stop.

"I can't believe how attracted I am to you," she says. "I'm usually fighting the guys off, not asking them to do stuff to me."

I don't respond, just continue to feel the soft skin of her taut body.

Her words and the way she says them sound more genuine than about anything else she has said, but I can't help but believe she has said them many, many times before.

It's surprising how much the instant, faux intimacy between us seems real. Destiny is not very bright and acts as though she's on something, but she doesn't come across as fake or disingenuous. She seems to be completely caught up in the moment, sexually aroused and available.

Though her skin and nipples are soft, the implants beneath are hard and feel every bit as artificial as they are.

The music, the dark, the sexually charged atmosphere, her words, the movement of her body, the smell of her perfumed-tinged sex all conspire to place me in a kind of hypnotic trance.

I move my hands to her small, tight ass and begin to rub it.

She leans back a little and pulls open the front of her bottoms. "Touch me," she says.

I do.

She moans breathlessly. "Can I come?" she asks. "I know we're supposed to be back here for you, but I'm so . . . hot and bothered. I'm not gonna charge you for any of this . . . any of these songs. I just want to come. I've never done this before. Never."

When she is finished, she says, "Do you want me to blow you? Or you can fuck me if you want to."

"Thank you," I say. "I really appreciate the offer and you're so beautiful and sexy, but I . . . I have to go."

"Really?"

"Got to be in court early in the morning," I say. "Very big case. Have to be my best."

"But—"

I move to stand and she climbs off me.

"I've already stayed longer than I should have," I say. "You're just so appealing I couldn't break away."

"Oh, okay. Well . . . Do you want my number? We should get together outside of here."

"Absolutely," I say.

She gives me her number and I put it in my phone. She pulls out her phone and waits for me to give her mine, which, against my better judgement, I do.

TWENTY-ONE

I'm feeling so guilty as I'm walking to my car, I don't notice the two men coming up behind me.

I'm parked in the far right corner of the dim back parking lot where Ashlynn told me there is no security camera coverage —some fifty yards from the back of the building. There are very few cars in this lot—most are in the front and on the side—and no one else is around.

"Hey, guy. Vat? You zink you just going to leave wizout paying piper?"

I turn to see two Russian guys approaching me. The one talking is a lean muscular man with closely cropped hair in his late twenties or early thirties. He's wearing an expensive black suit with a black silk shirt unbuttoned halfway down his chest. The huge guy with him is around the same age and is wearing an Adidas black track suit with three white stripes on the sides of the arms and legs.

As a convicted felon, it's against the law for me to carry a firearm. If I'm ever caught with one, I'll be sent back to prison, which is why I don't have one on me or in my vehicle.

"You the piper?" I ask.

"I vork for zee piper."

Track Suit says, "Vee are all zee piper."

Black Suit looks at him and smiles. "Yes. Exactly. Vee are all zee piper." Looking back at me, he says, "Eet ees disrespectful to come into our place of business, fuck one of our girls, and not pay. Zen just valtz right out vizout paying for pleasure."

They both speak with heavy Russian accents—replacing *i* with *ee*, randomly omitting the articles *a* and *the*, rolling their *r*'s, harshing their *h*'s, softening their *e*'s, and replacing their *th*'s with *z*'s and their *w*'s with *v*'s.

"I haven't fucked anyone," I say, "and I certainly haven't done any valtzing."

Black Suit laughs and looks at Track Suit. "Vee are dealing with tough guy here. Cool as cucumber. Not scared. Does not pay for sexy time and zen mocks us to our faces like vee are joke."

"Pretty sure he just mocked you," Track Suit says.

"He's rrright," I say, rolling the *r*. "I'll get to him eventually if I live long enough, but so far it has just been you."

Black Suit nods slowly, appreciatively, then slips his hand into his coat and comes out with a Glock that must have been in a shoulder holster there. At first glance I think it's the Glock 17, but upon closer inspection I think it's the slimmed down Glock 19, a compact, polymer-framed, semi-automatic 9mm.

"You not scared of us," Black Suit says. "You scared of zis?"

"I'd have to hold it and get a better look at it to tell you for sure."

He laughs again.

"Okay, guy, funny time ees over. You pay or vee shoot your dick off."

"I'm very fond of my dick," I say. "I'd like to keep it—not just keep it but keep it right where it is."

"So . . ."

"How much to keep it right where it is?" I ask.

"A grand, man."

"A thousand dollars to keep my dick where it is?" I say. "I mean, I'm not sayin' it's not worth that. It is. But . . ."

Before he can respond, Blade walks up.

"*Hey*," she says in an exaggerated tone, holding the word out for a long beat. "What's goin' down here?"

"What ze—" Track Suit starts to say.

"Nigger dyke," Black Suit explains. "Not many around here. You are actually seeing one een vild." Then to Blade he says, "Pussy inside club. You go zere now."

"Better do what he says," I say, "or he'll shoot your pussy off."

"That's what they're doing?" she says. "Shootin' your dick off. Must be a hell of a shot."

"Oh, nice," I say. "Dick jokes. Last thing I hear before havin' my dick shot off is a joke about my dick."

"You two know each—"

Before Black Suit can finish his sentence, Blade withdraws a switchblade from somewhere on her body, slices his wrist open, spins around behind him and slices a gash into Track Suits left leg.

Black Suit drops the Glock and falls to his knees grasping his wrist. Track Suit is already on the ground holding his leg with both hands.

"Stupid bitches brought guns to a knife fight," she says.

I grab the Glock off the asphalt as Blade unzips Track Suit's jacket and removes his from the shoulder holster there.

"Your wounds aren't fatal," Blade says, "but they will be if you don't get them patched up. Don't fuck around and bleed out. Go get them seen about."

"Hop in," I say to her. "I'll give you a ride to your vehicle."

She does and as we pull away, the two Russians are trying to get up.

"How'd you know to—"

"Ashlynn texted me," she says. "She could tell there'd be trouble."

"Is she okay?"

"Yeah. Says she'll explain everything when she comes to get Alana."

I pull up to her car, hand her Black Suit's Glock, and as she's getting out, I say, "Thank you."

"For saving your dick from getting shot off?" she says. "Not sure I did you any favors. That shit bound to keep gettin' your ass into trouble."

TWENTY-TWO

"Sounds like Dimitri," Ashlynn is saying. "He's Lev's nephew."

Ashlynn, Blade, Lexi, and I are in my living room. Alana is asleep on my bed. The door is slightly ajar so we can see her, and we are talking quietly. Ashlynn is back in street clothes but still has some glitter on her face and in her hair and she smells strongly of floral body lotion and cigarette smoke.

"Who's Lev?" Blade asks.

"The owner. The big guy with Dimitri would be Bogdan. He's a hired gun. Works for Lev some. Mostly works for Dimitri."

"I had no idea you were working for and around such dangerous people," I say.

"It's gotten worse lately. Lev's okay. He's older and a real gentleman. He's good to the girls. But Dimitri is . . . well, you saw. He's not . . . He really doesn't have anything to do with the club, but when Lev is away . . . he does what he wants—which is mostly shaking down the customers. He acts like he's some of the girls' pimp, but I don't think he really is. He does pimp some, but as far as I know not any girls working at

Cloud Nine. Lev has no tolerance for that sort of thing. No trickin', no drugs, no drama. But like I say . . . when he's away . . ."

"We've got to get you out of there," I say.

"I'm okay. I stay way away from Dimitri and all that. Keep my head down. Do my shift and get out of there."

"But even being that close to people like that. Does Dimitri know you have a connection to us?"

She shakes her head. "No one there but Miss Rachel, Declan, and Winston know anything about me at all." Miss Rachel is the house mom and Declan and Winston are bouncers.

"But—"

"They look out for me," she says. "Dimitri doesn't fuck with them."

"Still," I say. "It's too—"

"It could be a lot worse," she says. "Most other clubs are. Lev is good to us. Just gets a little . . . crunchy when he's not around. But it's the best and safest club around. And there's no straight job I can do that'd give me as much time with Alana or a fraction of the money."

"Y'all can move in here and—"

"And what?"

"You can go back to school."

"And when you go back to prison?" she asks. "What do we do then?"

"I'm not— I don't plan to go back to prison."

"Didn't plan on going the first time," she says. "I appreciate what you're . . . offering, but you're already doing too much for me and Alana. And the truth is . . . you're barely making it as it is. Everything is okay the way it is. Let's keep it that way."

Blade says, "You let us know if anybody gives you any trouble. Anybody. At all. And if the little dick shooter didn't get to the hospital in time, he won't be around to bother you or anyone else."

"They got sewn up," she says. "Lev has a doctor. He came and took care of it. But now they're gonna come after y'all. No way Dimitri or Bogdan let this go. I'm worried about y'all."

"We'll be okay," Blade says.

"Dimitri is dangerous," she says.

"Oh, he dangerous now he after us?" Blade says.

"Especially when he feels like he's been disrespected."

"Well, he was certainly that," Blade says. "And I got more to give him if he wants to come get some."

"I'm most worried about Burke," she says. "He can't carry a weapon."

"My hands are registered as lethal weapons," I say.

"Everybody call me Blade," Blade says. "Maybe we start callin' you Hands."

Lexi says, "I'm always armed, so when I'm around . . . And Blade's always armed."

"So now we just have to arm Alana and he'll be covered," Blade says.

"Or," I say, "I could just tell Logan that Dimitri and Bogdan are harassing his girlfriend and tryin' to turn her into a workin' woman, and maybe they take each other out."

"Ooh," Blade says. "I like that."

I tap my temple with my index finger. "Work smarter not harder."

"Hey, Hands," she says. "Careful not to hurt yourself with those lethal weapons."

TWENTY-THREE

"You okay?" Lexi asks.

Blade, Ashlynn, and Alana are gone and we are alone on the couch in my living room.

I nod.

"What is it?" she asks. "You've been acting different since you got back. Did the incident with Dimitri and Bogdan—"

"No," I say. "I feel . . . We haven't really defined what we are—and I'm not sayin' we need to. But I feel guilty for . . . tonight."

"Tonight?"

"Going to Cloud Nine."

"I told you to," she says.

"I know, but—"

"And it was for work," she says. "But even if it wasn't . . . I got no problem with you going to a titty bar."

"Okay. Good."

"You didn't fuck a stripper in the parking lot, did you?"

"I did not," I say.

"Okay then."

I start to tell her exactly what I did do but am unable.

"I did get a lap dance," I say.

"From Destiny?"

"Yeah. And I didn't have to—not to get the information that I needed."

"So you did it . . . because you wanted a lap dance?"

I shake my head. "It wasn't about her or the dance."

"Then why? Oh, because of Logan?"

"Yeah."

"I get that," she says. "I'd like to get a lap dance from his girlfriend too. Maybe next time we can go together."

I smile. "Thanks for . . . understanding."

At first I'm relieved and grateful that she's being so cool about it, but then I begin to wonder why. Is it because she doesn't care? Is it because of what or who she's been doing? Maybe I'm not the only probationer she's fucking. Or maybe I'm being paranoid and should just appreciate her reasoned response.

"You don't have to tell me what you did during the dance," she says. "I don't need the details."

"Okay."

"But if you want to," she says. "Or need to. It's okay."

"Thank you, but—"

"Actually," she says, standing and straddling me. "It's probably best if you just show me."

TWENTY-FOUR

"Whoa whoa whoa," Blade is saying. "You feel guilty for fingering a stripper?"

It's the next morning and we are driving back out to Flamingo South to interview Barbara Woodward, the retired schoolteacher and former neighbor of the Harrisons.

"It's not like that," I say.

"Then what's it like?"

"I feel bad for *why* I did it."

Her voice rises. "To get back at that piece of shit rapist who put you in prison and is blackmailing you?"

"I feel bad for using Destiny like that," I say.

"*Destiny?*" she says. "You don't even know her real name. She's playing a part. You didn't even use a real person—just a persona. She used you as much as you used her. But you know what . . . feel bad if it makes you feel better."

I start to respond but stop and think about what she's saying. Feeling bad about it does make me feel better. Is that all I'm doing—trying to make myself feel better about what I did? Punish myself with a little guilt so I can tell myself I'm really a good guy and not someone who'd normally do something like that?

"Just tell me you weren't stupid enough to say something to Lexi about it," she says.

I look at her and frown.

"*I knew it,*" she shouts. "I knew it. You . . . are . . . such a . . . Brah, who you need to feel bad for is *yo'self. You're* the reason you can't have nice things. Man . . . maybe I should've let 'em shoot your dick off last night."

Thankfully, we arrive at Flamingo South, so mercifully this conversation is forced to end—at least for now.

After we park and just before we get out, she says, "Any other shit you feel guilty about you wanna get off your chest?"

"Actually, there is," I say.

"Brah, I was kidding. Damn."

"I feel guilty that all the work we're getting is keeping us from working on Kaylee's case."

She nods and this time she frowns too. "Yeah, I feel bad about that shit too."

Barbara Woodward still lives in the same unit she did back in 2000 when Leah disappeared.

Her home smells of coffee, bacon, scrambled eggs, and sweet rolls, but none of those things are visible. Unlike the Harrisons' old unit, her small condo looks and feels like a home, not a rental that someone is living in temporarily.

"Still grieve for that little girl every day," she is saying. "Just breaks my heart."

She's a white-haired white woman in her seventies whose bottom half has gone soft and big while her top half has remained thinnish. Resembling an old glass Coke bottle, she has a flat, bony chest and a relatively small waist that blossoms into thick thighs and a large ass.

"Always felt bad for those kids," she says. "Hard having

young parents. Not that they were bad parents. They did their best, but being young and broke . . . Working all the time. Never having enough. Not even having figured out who you are yet and trying to help a child become who they are. Saw it all the time when I was teaching. I taught third grade for thirty-six years. Not in any way saying Heather and Malcolm were bad parents. They weren't. But . . . I tried to help out where I could. I did—and still do to a lesser extent—with all the kids who live here. Not in any big ways, but . . . in important ways. I always have healthy snacks around. Always give them a vitamin gummy. Always give them a hug and some encouraging words. And either read to them or have them read to me. It's not much, but—"

"It's a lot," I say. "Sounds like the kind of surrogate grandmother I could've used when I was coming up."

"Never had children of my own," she says, "but have always felt like I had hundreds of children over the years. My classroom was like a safe, positive place where a kid could escape from her or his worry and woes for a little while. I've always tried to make my home that same kind of place."

"What can you tell us about Leah or her family?"

"She was a sort of rough and tumble girl. Not a tomboy exactly—she had plenty of girliness to her nature—but she was high energy and tough and adventurous and very, very smart. She lacked some social grace for sure. Her parents weren't very . . . That kind of thing wasn't a priority for them. She was a little wild and rough around the edges—bluntly said what was on her mind. But she was also kind and could, at times, be very gentle and loving."

"So given her adventurous nature and energy and everything you just described," I say, "it sounds like it wouldn't be surprising for her to get up and go out of her condo."

"Except for it being a stormy night," she says. "She was

genuinely afraid of the dark and afraid of storms. I can't imagine what would cause her to do it when she did it. But otherwise, yes. She would certainly go out without her parents knowing it. They'd call or come down and say, 'Is Leah down there with you?'"

"Did you see her the night she disappeared?"

She nods. "The moment I heard about that absurd hurricane party, I knew Heather and Malcolm would be going. So I took the kids a snack and checked on them—not just the Harrison kids but all the ones I knew of whose parents would be at that party. But this was pretty early in the evening. As usual, Leah had Kyle doing all sorts of . . . they had built a blanket fort and were pretending all sorts of things. She was always a strong princess slaying dragons and rescuing the weak. They had a castle wall made of chairs and coffee tables and end tables that they could actually walk around to survey their kingdom. She had more creativity and imagination than about any other kid I've ever worked with. The official game of their kingdom was sock ball and they were playing it, using Kyle's bat to hit a pair of rolled up socks. I just knew they were going to break everything in the place, but I'll tell you this—they were having fun and everything was good. They were having far more fun than any of the other kids that night, which was generally par for the course. And it was because of Leah. She knew how to have fun. Kyle just went along with her."

"There was a school picture of another kid in her backpack," I say. "So far no one seems to know who it is. Was it one of your students or—"

"I've never seen it," she says. "I have no idea who it is."

Blade quickly pulls up a picture of the picture on her phone and shows it to Barbara.

She studies it for a long moment the shakes her head. "You know how the population is around here. I usually only had two or three African American students in my class each year. I'd remember her if I had had her as a student."

"You ever see Leah with this pic or she ever mention a friend or pen pal or anything that might be related to it?" Blade asks.

She seems to think about it then shakes her head. "Not that I recall. It's strange, isn't it, that no one has identified her in twenty years."

"Especially given how much this picture has been circulated and shown online," I say.

"A real mystery," she says.

"One of many," I say. "Do you have any ideas or theories about what might have happened that night? Anyone you suspect of being involved—her parents or another neighbor or anyone?"

"Living next to people and interacting with them for as long as I did the Harrisons, you get to know them—especially when you go into their home and they come into yours. Heather and Malcolm had their issues, but never, not for one moment, did I ever suspect them of having anything to do with whatever happened to their daughter. They adored her and were good to her and to Kyle—as good as they knew how and were capable of. Whatever happened to her . . . her family didn't have anything to do with it, and I can't think of any of the neighbors I knew at the time who could have either. But . . . it's a big building with lots of people living in it and lots of transient guests coming and going. Could've easily been one of them."

TWENTY-FIVE

Sadie Arnold is a physical therapist who works at Bay Medical Center or Sacred Heart or Ascension or whatever they call it these days. It has grown and expanded and gone through name changes, but it will always be Bay to me, just as the other hospital in town will always be Gulf Coast.

Sadie, who was Leah's playmate at Flamingo South when they were kids, is now a young mother in her early thirties with shoulder-length coarse, dark blond hair and almond-shaped brown eyes.

She is meeting us downtown on her lunch break and is wearing dark blue scrubs and has her hair pulled back in a ponytail.

"I was only there some of the time," she is saying. "My folks had just split and that was Dad's bachelor pad. We weren't super close but we played together a good bit."

We are sitting at a table in the courtyard of Millie's having lunch while we talk, since this is Sadie's only chance to eat during her shift.

I'm having the crab cakes, which are delicious. Blade is

having fried gator, and Sadie is having a spinach salad and a bowl of spicy seafood gumbo.

The mid-October day is pleasant—thanks mostly to a drop in the humidity—and there's a nice breeze. Behind us, in and around the enormous oaks of McKenzie Park, the disembodied voices of birds can be heard above the flowing waters of the fountains.

"Dad can probably tell you more than I can," she says. "I was a self-involved kid whose parents just divorced. I remember I liked her. She was fun. But I also was a little . . . I couldn't match her energy or . . . I don't know what to call it . . . her . . . She was always getting into stuff. Sort of relentless that way. She was fun to play with for a while, but she always wore me out. She wanted to keep going, but I'd have to have a break. She also . . . I wouldn't have known how to say this at the time . . . but, she lacked boundaries. She'd just show up at our place, walk right in if the door wasn't locked. She was a little wild and didn't have a ton of supervision. I'm sure none of this helps but it's what I remember."

"It helps," I say. "Everything we can learn about Leah from back then—and the condo and the people who lived there—all helps tremendously."

She finishes her salad and takes a few bites of her gumbo.

"I'm not sure I can tell you anything else," she says after taking a sip of her water.

"Were there any other kids y'all played with?" I ask.

She seems to think about it. "Not consistently. Sometimes we'd hang out with the tourist kids, but not much. And not that late in the season. We did play with—well, he wasn't a kid, just acted like one. A developmentally delayed teenager from one of the townhomes just down from us. Arthur something. He was like seventeen or eighteen but he acted younger than we did.

We made a fort out of a storage shed behind his house sometimes."

"That's the place Leah broke into the night she disappeared," I say.

"She did?"

"Yeah. You didn't know?"

"I don't really know anything about any of it. I was a kid. Just knew she disappeared that night. Never really looked into it as an adult. Didn't think there was much to look into. Always thought either someone snatched her or she got pulled out into the Gulf by the storm."

"Any idea why she'd leave her home that night?" I ask.

She shakes her head. "But it doesn't surprise me. Like I said, she was always doing stuff like that. She was probably pretending she was a storm chaser or something."

Blade says, "We were told she was scared of the dark and of storms."

"I don't think she was scared of anything, but . . . I . . . Maybe I'm misremembering. Like I say, I was a kid. But we went out plenty at night and she never mentioned being scared."

"What about the things in her backpack?" I ask. "Do you know the significance of any of them?"

"What was in her backpack?" she asks.

I show her pictures on my phone.

She studies the photo.

It's a picture of the items—two outfits, a library copy of *The Secret Garden*, a notebook, a pencil, a teddy bear, a pink Power Ranger action figure, a magic 8-ball, a blue Nintendo Gameboy Advance SP, and a school picture of another little girl—displayed on top of the backpack itself.

She shrugs. "Don't know. Seems like pretty random stuff."

"Do you know who this little girl is?" I ask.

She shakes her head again. "Who is she?"

"Nobody seems to know," Blade says.

"We're wondering if maybe this picture was used in an early kind of analog catfishing scheme," I say. "A predator pretending to be this little girl maybe."

"Oh, wow. Interesting. Guess it could be, but . . . Occam's razor would say that it's a picture some tourist family from way far away left in a room or on the beach and Leah picked it up. She probably invented an entire story around it—the other girl was in trouble and Leah had to save her. Something like that. But she never showed it to me."

Blade says, "Any creeps in the building? Anybody ever try to mess with y'all or—"

"My dad was very protective of me. You'd probably have to ask him. There were places he told me not to go, people he told me to stay away from, but he didn't say why and I didn't ask. Mostly just did what he said. Thinking back now . . . yeah . . . I didn't realize it at the time, but he was probably telling me who to steer clear of and which condos to avoid because they were pervs. I'm sure he could tell you."

"Well, let's hope so," Blade says. "We talk to him next."

TWENTY-SIX

"This is going to sound terrible . . ." Erik Arnold is saying, "but I really didn't want Sadie playing with the Harrison kids."

Erik Arnold is a dermatologist with a practice on Jenks close to Gulf Coast Regional Medical Center.

He's a tall, trim, early fifties man with a full head of hair and a neatly trimmed beard, both of which are dyed dark brown to match his eyes.

We are in his office in the back right corner of the building. He's behind his large desk and Blade and I are in the two chairs across from it.

"I'm not sayin' they were bad kids," he continues. "Just . . . a little . . . They were little heathens—not a lot of manners, not a lot of parental supervision, always getting into stuff. Not bad stuff, but . . . stuff. The brother wasn't quite as bad as the sister, but . . . She'd just walk into my condo without asking. She'd help herself to whatever was in my fridge or . . . anything else she wanted. Like it was her house. She acted like she felt more comfortable there than Sadie did. The point is . . . I didn't encourage their relationship. Sadie still played with her some, but not much. So she was around a little. I knew her some, but not very well. We were all sad when she vanished, but . . . not like if we had been real close."

I nod. Beside me, Blade gives no reaction.

"I had just gotten a divorce," he says, "and my ex didn't want Sadie coming to my place, didn't think I could take good care of her. I didn't want anything going wrong and I thought if anything was going to go wrong it would be with that wild child, Leah Harrison. I thought Sadie might break an arm doing one of Leah's stunts or get hurt in some other way or lost or . . . something, and Jill would use that against me, keep her from coming to see me."

"The Harrisons were poor, weren't they?" Blade says. "Hell, they still are."

"Had nothing to do with that," he says. "I had no idea of their financial situation. They were living in the same condominium as me, so . . ."

"But you could tell," she says. "The way their kids dressed and talked and acted. You knew."

"I'm telling you it didn't have anything to do with that. I had just been cleaned out by my ex. I wasn't in good shape myself."

"Any other reasons why your ex didn't want Sadie at your place?" Blade asks.

"It was just her way of busting my balls," he says, "being in control. Getting back at me."

"For what?"

"Sorry?"

"Getting back at you for what?" she asks.

She's found something.

"For sleeping around."

"While y'all were married?"

"Some, yeah. And she certainly didn't want me having any fun after we divorced."

"You sleep with her sister or her best friend or something?"

"*No*. She doesn't have a sister."

"But if she did . . ."

"I did sleep with one of her friends. Not a close friend, but . . ."

"Is that why your daughter who's a nurse works at the hospital instead of your practice?"

"No. She wants to be more medically challenged than being a dermatologist's nurse."

"Back in the day . . . your new bachelor condo was a real pussy pad, right?" she says.

"No, that's not how I'd—"

"I understand you were very popular with the ladies at Flamingo South," she says.

As far as I know, no one had said anything like that.

He shrugs and gives a little wry, self-satisfied smirk.

"You ever mess around with Heather Harrison?" she asks.

"No."

His *no* is not very emphatic. Blade is onto something.

"No? Beautiful young poet. Married beneath herself. Looking to trade her blue-collar cook in for a doctor."

"Look, there were some wild parties back then and the Harrisons were involved in some of them. We were all young and horny and living there was like being on vacation. And there was always a new group of people coming through. We were all doin' what young people do. And it was mostly as a group, not like an affair."

"We talkin' orgies?" she says.

"Just group parties."

"Sex parties," she says.

"If I slept with Heather—and I say *if*—I was one of many.

But whether I did or not has nothing to do with her daughter's disappearance."

"Unless you know what happened to her," she says, "you have no way of knowing that. Do you know what happened to her?"

TWENTY-SEVEN

"Sex parties and shit," Blade says. "Sounds like the Harrisons used to be down to clown."

We are back in the car headed toward St. Andrews for me to meet with Clyde Broussard.

I nod. "We need to find out what happened at the hurricane party the night Leah went missing."

"The host and some of the attendees are on our list."

"Cool."

"You figured out what you gonna tell Clyde?" she asks.

"Not exactly."

"Do me a favor and try to refrain from tellin' him you fingered Logan's girlfriend experience."

I laugh. "Will do."

"You should sic Logan on Dimitri like you said."

"He'd just have Clyde deal with them and that's one against two."

"I didn't do so bad the other night when it was me against them. Clyde can handle himself. Why you worried about him?"

"I—"

"You like him?"

"I guess I do. I respect him. I think he tries to do the right thing. But even if I'm wrong, I don't want to set him up. I'm not going to lie to him."

"You feeling guilty about pittin' Logan against Dimitri?"

"Some, I guess, but mainly I don't want any collateral damage—especially Destiny or Clyde."

"You one in a million, you know that? One of 'em sent your ass to prison and is blackmailing you into bein' his bitch and the other is coming to kill you, but you feel bad about havin' them take each other out."

CLYDE and I meet at the St. Andrews Marina.

We're standing at the rail looking out at the bay.

It's just the two of us. Blade is in the car and if anyone came with Clyde, they're not visible.

"I haven't finished my investigation yet," I say, "but I don't think Destiny is having an affair."

He looks at me, his eyebrows arching. "Really?"

"Affair implies a relationship," I say.

"Ah," he says, nodding slowly and looking back out at the bay.

"I don't want her getting hurt," I say.

"Me either," he says.

"She's giving him an experience. It's probably all she has to give. What does he think he's getting?"

He shrugs.

"What's he giving?" I say. "Does he really want a girl-friend? I figured she was just a beard for his perverted and predatory activities."

He doesn't say anything.

We pass a moment in silence.

Eventually, I say, "You know the owner of Cloud Nine?"

"Lev?" he says.

"His nephew, Dimitri, is tryin' to play pimp to some of the dancers," I say. "Destiny is one of them."

He faces me again. "Got her turnin' tricks?"

"No. Shaking down customers when his uncle isn't around. Jumped me in the parking lot. If I carry I go back to prison, so I was unarmed."

"You in the wrong profession to go out naked."

"I know. Blade came along and saved my ass."

He nods. "She a badass bitch."

"You gonna tell Logan about Dimitri?" I ask.

He nods.

"He gonna send you after him?"

"Probably."

"Be careful. He works with a big guy named Bogdan."

"Thanks. I appreciate that."

"Blade cut them both up pretty good," I say. "They'll be coming for us."

"You should carry," he says. "I can hook you up with some untraceable hardware. Better to be popped and go back to prison than get popped and put in the ground."

"How much juice does Lev have?" I ask.

"Some."

"Somethin' happens to Dimitri," I say, "he got big guns he can bring in?"

He nods. "Russian mob."

"That's what I was afraid of. Neither of us need that kind of trouble."

"'Specially your skinny white ass walkin' around unprotected."

"Maybe not mention this to Logan for now," I say. "See if we can figure somethin' else out."

"Like what?"

"Can you give me a couple of days to try to figure that out?"

TWENTY-EIGHT

Reginald and Valarie Scott, who go by Reg and Val, own a mom-and-pop pizza joint in an old storefront strip mall not far past the curve on Thomas Drive.

Off-season they are only open for lunch, so we meet with them in the late afternoon as they are cleaning up.

The small pizzeria, which only serves takeout, is essentially a counter with a large commercial pizza oven behind it, and smells of garlic and butter and onion and tomato sauce and baking bread. The counter, which has a plexiglass shield above it, normally displays the pizzas on offer, but now sits empty except for the cash register at the far end.

Though in their mid-forties, they seem younger. Trim, stylish, energetic, and covered in flour after a full shift of preparing and serving large thin-crust pies.

As young and vibrant as they seem now, I can only imagine how they must have seemed to Leah when they were her neighbors.

"We made y'all one of our specialties," Reg is saying.

"Thank you very much," I say.

"Figured y'all could have it for dinner. Reheating instructions are on the box."

"Really appreciate that."

"Pleasure. Hope y'all like it. Mind if we keep cleaning while we talk? We're on a tight schedule today."

"No problem. We appreciate you talking to us."

"Happy to help," Val says. "We've been thinking and talking about back then since you called. Not sure what we remember will be any help, but we'll tell you what we know."

"What do you remember about Leah?" I ask.

"She was a cool combination of sweet and spunky," Val says. "So much personality packed into that little body."

"We never had kids," Reg says. "We're really not the parenting kind, but she and her brother and a few of the other kids really seemed to love coming to our place."

"I always enjoyed having them," Val says. "I was trying to figure out the appeal. I think it was that we were adults but young, that we didn't have kids of our own, that we treated them more like adults than children."

"Our place was always clean," Reg adds, "and we always had snacks. We never locked our doors. Nobody did back then. The kids could come and go as they wanted, but it was mostly just Leah."

"We didn't know much about their home life, but I gathered there might be some chaos or contention they were trying to get away from. I don't know for sure and none of it seemed severe, but . . . there was a certain tranquil vibe to our unit that may have been missing from theirs."

"Don't get her wrong, we weren't sitting around all Zen and shit," Reg says. "We were young and wild—still are, well still wild, not so young any longer—but when the kids came over, we put our wild ways up for a few and hung out with them."

"What kind of wild shit you have to put up?" Blade asks.

"We didn't drink or smoke or do any drugs when they were around," he says. "We put on clothes, turned off the porn. That kind of shit."

"Do you recall the last time you saw Leah?" I ask.

"I saw her on the day she went missing," Val says. "In the afternoon. Not for long, but . . . she seemed like she always did. Happy. Talkative. Enjoying herself. Into something. She was always into something—some adventure or game or toy or idea. Her little mind was amazing—and so creative. If the reason she left in the middle of the night in that storm was because something was wrong or she was upset, it had to have happened after about three that afternoon because she was absolutely fine then."

"I can't recall the last time I saw her," Reg says. "A day or two before her death I'd say."

"*Death?*" Blade says. "You know something we don't?"

"We all know what it is," he says. "A kid that age can't run off to start a new life somewhere. And if the storm didn't get her, I hope she's dead instead of in some pedophile's dungeon suffering a living hell."

We are all silent a moment in the echo of his unsettling words.

"But let me be clear," he adds after a moment. "I have no knowledge of what happened to her or where she is. I was just saying what we all know. It wasn't a confession."

"What can you tell us about Leah's parents?" I ask.

"They were the most like us of anyone who lived in the Flamingo," Val says. "We . . . were into some of the same things."

"Such as?"

She smiles. "Essentially sex, drugs, and rock 'n roll. We'd've done more with them if they hadn't had kids."

"Were they good parents?" I ask.

"Very good, I thought," she says. "Considering their age and experience and what they came from. Don't think they had a lot of good examples coming up."

"Did y'all go to the hurricane party that night?" I ask.

They nod.

"What sort of party was it?" I ask.

"What do you mean?" Reg asks.

"We understand there were a lot of sex parties back then," I say. "Just wondered if this was one of them."

"Every party is a sex party," he says. "Whether you're hookin' up with someone new or going home and fuckin' who you went to the party with. But in terms of group sex parties . . . there were some back then. The kind where you knew you were going to an orgy and that's why you were going. Some were the *Shortbus* kind where you bring a partner and fuck them while everyone else is fuckin' theirs. Others were sort of key parties, so random partnerings. Others were pairing off and going somewhere private. And a few were old-school orgies— everybody fucking everybody."

"Which kind was the hurricane party?"

"It was just a hurricane party, but like I say, all parties are sex parties. There was definitely some hookin' up going on. Plenty of good drugs. And everybody had the next day off, so . . ."

"How were Malcolm and Heather that night?"

"Wasted and rollin'," he says. "We all were. Always were at Victor's parties."

"They seemed more out of it than normal though," Val says. "Don't you think? They were usually pretty good about not overdoing it since they had the kids to take care of—or getting a babysitter if they were going to."

"Tells us about Victor," Blade says.

"He was a creep," Val says.

"It was his party," Reg says. "We only went to his parties because of the volume of good drugs and alcohol. It was the only way he could get people to attend. And it wasn't at his place."

"What does that mean?" Blade says.

"No matter how good his shit was, most of us refused to go to his place," Reg says. "Too many people had woken up there with no memory of the night before too many times. He knew none of us would come, so he threw it down by the pool."

"It was really cool," Val says. "Dark and windy and—you could feel the storm coming in."

"Anything bad or out of the ordinary happen?" I ask.

Reg shakes his head.

Val says, "Nothin' out of the ordinary. Always have a few issues when there's that much drinking and partying. Some dick measuring between some of the men. Some jealous outbursts—especially if someone's partner hooked up with someone they felt threatened by. Or just if they weren't able to find a match and their partner did."

"Any of that with the Harrisons?" I ask.

"There was never any of that kind of shit from Heather," she says. "But . . . Malcolm was always getting a little upset or jealous about something. Never any big deal, but it was clear he knew she was a settler and he was a reacher."

"None of this has anything to do with Leah or her disappearance," Reg says. "There were no kids there. Never were. And they kept all of this out of their home."

"We won't know what has anything to do with Leah's disappearance until we find it," I say. "We've got to gather as much information as we can. Everything matters until it doesn't. And we appreciate your help."

"We're happy to help," Val says.

"Just don't want to waste your time with—" Reg's phone

rings and he pulls it out and looks at it. "Sorry. I need to take this."

He answers the call as he walks into the back.

As soon as he's out of the room, Val moves over closer to us and lowers her voice.

"Malcolm was with me the night Leah vanished. No one knows but the original detective on the case. He said he'd keep it a secret if he could, and he did. Always felt bad for Malcolm. He's a good guy. Heather's just . . . out of his league. Reg and I have always been mostly open about things, but it bothers him and he . . . well, he always sort of identified with Malcolm and I knew he'd know why I slept with him—"

"Out of pity," Blade says.

"That was part of it."

"And that's part of why you're with Reg," I say.

She shakes her head. "I'd never put it like that, but I am attracted to a certain type of man. We all have types, right? A certain amount of insecurity and underdogness, among other things, does it for me."

"Hey," Blade says, "there are tops and there are bottoms. Got to have both."

"Exactly," she says. "And that was the problem. Heather was the top in their relationship but she's really a bottom. Every other man I ever saw her hook up with was an alpha and dominated her—but only in bed. She's always gonna be smarter and more dominant everywhere else. At least she was until . . ."

TWENTY-NINE

"Hey, it was a wild time," Victor says. "We were all young, dumb, and full of cum. Wouldn't trade it for the world."

Victor Dunkel is short and fat with bad skin, long fingernails, and a patch of long, thick, curly hair on the back of his otherwise bald head. He's pale with red splotches—some of which are flaking.

He works at a discount furniture warehouse in Lynn Haven, which at the moment is dead. We are standing with him in the far back corner between some lopsided recliners and mismatched mattresses.

"It was all about having a good time," he says. "We drank too much, did too many drugs, but no one got hurt and—"

"A ten-year-old girl vanished off the face of the earth," Blade says.

"None of us had anything to do with that," he says. "I thought you were asking what the adults got up to. I can't tell you anything about the kids. I didn't have kids and they never came to any of our . . . get-togethers. There were a lot of other people living in that building at the time and tons of tourists coming and going. I can't tell you anything about any of them. But our little group . . . We were good people just having a good time. And it was a different time, let me tell you. It was safe and . . . none of us locked our doors. Even if we had . . . members of the group had a key to each other's places, but . . . we didn't need them. We were young and liked to party."

"You threw the party that night, right?" I ask.

He shrugs. "I guess. I was probably the first one to say let's have a hurricane party, but we all . . . It was always a group effort."

"You provided the booze and the drugs?"

"Some of them—maybe even most, but people always brought their own shit too."

"Did anything out of the ordinary happen?" I ask.

He twists his thick blue lips and shakes his head slowly.

"Anyone act different or strange or anything?"

He shakes his head again. "Not at all. I mean, we all got fucked up, but there was nothing different or strange about that. I'm tellin' you, man, you're sniffin' around the wrong crotch. Nobody had anything to do with what happened to Heather's little girl. So . . . so tragic, but . . . unrelated."

"We ain't sniffin' 'round nobody's crotch," Blade says.

"And it *is* related," I say, "even if it's just what led to the parents being incapacitated and unable to protect and care for their child."

"Oh," he says. "Well, I guess . . . if you . . . But I wouldn't put it that way. And I wouldn't blame young parents having a good time for what happened to their daughter. They didn't leave the complex. They didn't get too wasted. And they went back up to their apartment pretty early. Hard to ask for much more than that."

"You still in touch with anyone from back then?"

He shakes his head. "Was another life."

"But you liked them?"

"Oh, yeah. It was a good group."

"Did you have a partner at the time?"

He shakes his head again. "Free as a bird."

"Who were you hookin' up with?" I ask.

"We all sort of slept with each other . . . so . . . different woman at different times."

"Heather Harrison?" I ask.

He frowns. "The one that got away. I really . . . It was just never in the cards for us. I actually . . . thought it might happen that night, but it didn't. Then after . . . what happened that night . . . they never came back to any of our . . . gatherings."

Blade says, "Nothin' like losing a child to fuck up your party vibe."

"I mean, sure, I get it," he says. "It was . . . tragic. They were never the same. I just . . . I was just disappointed. Heather Harrison was like a bucket list item for me. That's all."

"Leah's disappearance as inconvenient as hell for you, wasn't it?" Blade says.

"There's no need to be— I've got to get back to work. I've told you what I know. Sorry I couldn't be more helpful, but I just don't know anything."

THIRTY

"When something like this happens," Heather Harrison is saying, "it causes you to question everything. Everything. Every choice. Every decision. Every perception. Every assumption."

I am back on the balcony with Heather, back on uncomfortable plastic band patio chairs, back in the gravitational pull of the black hole of her grief.

It's late afternoon and the sun is sinking behind the clear green Gulf at the horizon, fiery red and orange plunging into the bubbling sea, a blacksmith's blade pulled from the forge and thrust into the waiting quenchant.

Today, in addition to her journal and phone, the small low round table between us holds a tattered paperback edition of Sylvia Plath's *Unabridged Journals*.

"I used to think there was some kind of order to the universe," she says. "Now I've seen behind that facade to the chaos beyond. Not just chaos, but . . . cruelty and capriciousness."

I don't say anything, just listen.

"Most people catch only glimpses of the absurdity and

inanity in passing," she continues. "It's much easier to either ignore or at least convince yourself those are the exceptions to the rule when that's all you see. But when you see the complete horror of the full catastrophe of this nightmare, you can no longer pretend the veil of order is anything but an illusion."

I don't necessarily disagree with her, but the contrast between what she's describing and the breathtaking beauty and majesty of the scene before us is stark. The setting sun has turned the sky above and beyond it a soft flamingo-pink and the Gulf below it sherbet-orange, and imbued the atmosphere with a gentle, hushed calm.

"I wasn't a bad mother, but I wasn't . . . I was young and stupid and self-involved. We didn't party a ton, didn't fuck around a lot, but . . . there's not a single thing I wouldn't do differently if I could."

She is so small, so diminutive and childlike even now, that back when she was a young mother she must have seemed like a child herself.

"My sexuality is completely shut down and has been since that night," she adds, "but back then I was . . . I can remember leaving parties early, not hookin' up with someone so I could get back to the kids—and resenting it. Or . . . not being happy about it. Feeling . . . Doing it out of duty."

This is the part I've been waiting for. I knew she'd get here eventually. I had shared with her what we had learned so far, what the others had been saying. Like before, she didn't need any additional prompting—only active listening.

"If I could go back, I'd never leave her side. Never go to a single stupid party. Never . . . I only ever got involved with a few guys—Erik and Reg and a couple of others—never Victor's creepy little ass, never anyone like him. Never anywhere near what was on offer. Always felt so righteous about that, about all the invitations I declined, about how I could've gotten up to so much more than I did. How absurd . . . to take pride in . . . I was so naive and restless, so . . . imperceptive. Doesn't matter now. Nothing does. But that doesn't keep me from obsessively scrutinizing my every action. What else am I going to do? Live my life? I don't have one. I vanished that night too."

"I know I can't begin to fathom what you're feeling, what you've been through," I say. "I know I know nothing and do not have any right to say anything, but . . ."

She turns and looks at me.

"If the world is chaotic and capricious and there's no order . . . you . . . can be no more to blame for what happened to Leah than I am. In the absence of order . . . there's no causality. Everything is random. You can't be responsible for something you never had any control over, can you?"

Her eyes glisten and she looks back out at the Gulf as the last visible vestiges of the setting sun, the curving, shimmering slice of rim sinks into the sea.

"Wouldn't it be pretty to think so," she says, referencing one of Hemingway's most famous lines.

"I know they're just words," I say, "and it's not like a logical argument is going to change anything, but . . . I just . . . I can see raging against the randomness or blaming yourself for not preventing it, but . . . not both. You can only be responsible if there is order. If there's only chaos, then . . . what could you have done?"

We are silent for a long moment.

Eventually she says, "Thank you. That may be the kindest most helpful thing anyone has said to me since . . . Who are you?"

"Nobody," I say. "A convicted felon with a library card."

"I don't believe I was with anyone that night," she says. "I . . . guess I can't be certain because I remember very little, but . . . my plan had been to stay at the party for a short while and go back and be with the kids since . . . Leah was so scared of bad weather. And I think that's what I did. I thought that's what Malcolm planned to do too—and I think he did come back eventually, but . . . I think Val is right. I think he was with her that night—at least most of it. I just don't remember much and I have to live with that. My little girl was going through . . . God knows what, and I was way past wasted."

THIRTY-ONE

That night I'm looking through Kaylee's case when Ashlynn calls.

I'm not doing much—just reading through the old case file and searching online for the latest posts and threads by the citizen sleuths and armchair internet detectives obsessed with her case.

"Malcolm Harrison is trashed and about to get his ass handed to him at the club," she says.

"I thought you were off tonight. Where is Alana?"

"I am. I'm not there. We're at home. One of the other girls texted me."

"Okay. Thanks. I'll go get him."

"Can you send someone else?" she asks. "Dimitri and Bogdan are there."

WHEN I WALK into Cloud Nine, Winston says, "Glad as hell to see you."

"That's a warm reception—even for a titty bar," I say.

"Look, go around to the side door and I'll have Declan bring him out. We don't need for Dimitri to see you. Declan and I ain't tryin' to lose our jobs over keepin' your ass alive."

I walk out the front door that a moment before I had walked in, get my car, and pull around to the side.

In another moment, the side door swings open and Declan steps through it sideways, half carrying Malcolm Harrison.

Once they are out, Declan kicks the door shut behind him.

I get out and open the passenger door and help get Malcolm inside.

"Thank you," I say when I close the door.

"We all feel bad for the guy," Declan says. "Unless he killed his kid."

"Haven't found anything to suggest that," I say.

"He usually pretty chill, just like all sad and shit, but tonight he started buggin' like a bitch."

When I join Malcolm in the car he is crying.

"Did Heather send you?" he says.

"Friend of mine works here," I say.

"Sorry for . . . this. Thanks for . . . You can drop me at my car. I'll sleep in it 'til I'm able to drive."

"I'm not gonna leave you to sleep in your car," I say. "I'll drive you home. You can call me when you get up in the morning and I'll come get you and take you back to your car."

I pull around the back of the building, through the parking lot where Dimitri and Bogdan had tried to shake me down, and take a right on the side street.

"I'm . . . not even all that drunk. I . . . just . . . I got upset."

"What happened?"

"Nothing happened. Nobody did anything or anything like that. I was just sittin' there gettin' a dance from this attractive young woman and I . . . it hit me that Leah would be older than her now, and I just . . . started freaking out."

"I understand."

"I'm not a creep or a pervert or anything," he says. "I'm just . . . lonely. And so fuckin' sad all the time. Heather thinks I've moved on. I haven't. I mean, I guess I have compared to her. I . . . I function a little, I guess. I mean, I work, but that's about it. I just want to be touched, to feel some fuckin' warmth from another human being, but . . . then I started thinking about Leah and all she's missed and how old she'd be now—older than we were when we lost her. And I just . . . came unglued. I had to get out of there. I . . . It was like I was having a panic attack. I wasn't tryin' to leave without paying. I wasn't. I wouldn't."

"They know that," I say. "Everyone understands."

"I don't think they do. They treated me like a . . . Like I was . . . I can never show my face in there again—not that I would ever want to."

"It's all okay," I say. "I'll make sure everyone understands. They'll get it. But you don't have to go back in there ever again if you don't want to."

Wanting to keep him talking, I don't ask where he wants me to take him, just continue driving through the quiet back streets of the residential area between 98 and Beach Drive.

"Heather won't touch me," he says. "Hasn't in two decades. She used to be so . . . She was really into me—at least physically. We touched all the time. And not just sexually. Like affection too. Held hands and rubbed shoulders and stuff. Always touching. Now . . . she can't even look at me for very long. Let alone touch me."

"What about Val Scott or any of the women from back in the day?"

He starts crying again. "I feel so fuckin' guilty, so . . . That I was fuckin' her while my little girl was being . . . I can't . . . I can't get it up. I've tried. I just can't. Makes me feel so . . . I feel guilty for even tryin' to be with any of them and I feel like a . . . weak, impotent loser 'cause I can't . . . because my limp dick just lays there all flaccid and— Stop the car."

He starts unbuckling his seatbelt and opening the door before I can pull over and stop.

Stumbling out of the car, he falls to the ground and begins to vomit.

I put the car in Park and jump out to check on him.

My car is only halfway on the shoulder, but there is no traffic.

We're in an old neighborhood of small pre-war homes on small lots. The little red brick and clapboard houses are so close to the street that it's like we're in someone's front yard.

When I reach the ditch, he's crying and dry heaving, the contents of his stomach expelled on the cold, damp ground in front of him.

"I can't keep livin' like this," he says. "I—"

A black SUV squeals up and screeches to a halt as someone inside starts shooting at us.

I grab Malcolm and pull him toward the open passenger door as rounds ricochet around us.

A nearby mailbox flag pings as a round hits it and the tip of the red hat of a ceramic gnome explodes.

Malcolm is confused and unsteady but doesn't resist.

When we reach my car, I dive inside and pull him in with me, yelling for him to close the door as I climb into the driver's seat.

As rounds begin to strike my car, I hear Dimitri yell something.

I slam the car in Drive and stomp on the gas, leaning down in the seat, staying low.

Malcolm nearly falls out as he tries to close the passenger door, but I grab his arm and hold onto him as he closes the door.

Dimitri and Bogdan give chase, continuing to fire rounds at us as they do.

"Duck down," I say. "Stay down."

"What the fuck is . . . Who is shooting at us?"

"Two guys from the club. Don't ever go back in there."

A round strikes the passenger side mirror, shattering the glass and putting a hole in the plastic behind it.

"What're we gonna do?" he says. "Do you have a gun?"

"No."

"Can you outrun them?"

"No."

"What are we gonna do?"

I roll through a four-way stop and take a left at the next intersection.

Because we're on a residential street and because I can't risk so much as a speeding ticket, I'm not driving very fast and they are right on our ass.

"Did you hear me?" Malcolm says. "What are we gonna do?"

"Just stay down and try to—"

I had assumed he had emptied his stomach back in the ditch, but I was wrong. He begins to lurch and spasm and heave, vomiting then hacking then spitting into my floorboard.

"Sorry," he says.

I pull out my phone and call Pete.

"Where are you?" I ask when he answers.

"Home. Why?"

I tell him what's happening.

"I can meet you," he says, "but there's probably a deputy closer. Let me see who's working tonight."

He puts me on hold.

When he comes back, he says, "Drive downtown. A deputy will be at Beach and 6th with his lights flashing. Just pull up beside him. If they back off and disappear, he'll follow you where you're going. If they engage, we'll call in the calvary, but that means involving more people."

I take a right at the next street, drive down to Beach and take a left.

Beach Drive is dark and quiet, with very little traffic. To our left, the remodeled mansions and the old oaks in front of them are lit by well-positioned spotlights, while to our right, the slight sliver of moon is reflected on the dark, gently undulating bay below.

When we're within a few hundred yards of the intersection of Beach and 6th, the deputy's lights can be seen.

Behind us, the SUV peels off, taking a left down the nearest side street between two of the large, stately old homes facing the bay.

THIRTY-TWO

When I walk into our office the next morning, Blade says, "Guess whose check bounced?"

"Ours? Mine? Am I getting warm?"

"Mr. Money Bags," she says.

"That's definitely not me or us," I say.

"Mr. Florida Lottery himself," she adds.

"Iversen?" I ask.

She nods. "Just got off the phone with the bank. It's no mistake. Bastard's broke as hell."

"All that talk about using his money for good . . ." I say.

"Appears what he used it for most was experimental cancer treatments in other countries."

"Why hire us to find Leah if he—"

"Let's go ask his gray ass," she says. "We'll take my whip since yours got shot the fuck up."

WE FIND Richard Iversen sitting on a cement bench in front of his wife's grave in Greenwood cemetery.

If possible, he looks even worse than before, both gaunter and grayer.

He no longer smells of chemo.

The burial plot, which is bordered by granite posts and filled with gravel, holds both his and his wife's graves. Beside hers, his headstone is already filled out with everything but the death date.

It's located in the back left corner of the sprawling cemetery near a small stand of scrub oaks and a few random planted palms still leaning from Hurricane Michael.

To our right beyond the leaning and rusted high chain-link fence is a railroad track and the back of some industrial buildings. Beyond the fence to our left is the back of an apartment complex.

He looks up at us when we walk up. "Have you found her?"

"Not yet," I say.

"Oh."

"Your check bounced," Blade says.

"Oh," he says again, nodding slowly.

"You don't seem surprised," she says.

"That's happening more and more these days."

"You out of money," she says.

He nods again. "What I'm really out of is time. I . . . haven't been keeping up with anything else, including money, for a while now. Just been spending and not tracking. Never thought I'd outlive my money."

His voice is so soft and weak it's hard to hear him.

"Burned through most of it tryin' to buy more time," he says, then nods at his headstone. "Trying to push back that second date as far as possible. All I did was . . . waste the little time I had."

"Your ass knew you were broke when you hired us," Blade says.

"I didn't know," he says. "Not for sure. But . . . you're right. I suspected."

"What, you hopin' we'd find out what happened to her before the check bounced?"

"I'm not a good . . . My wife was, but . . . I've been tryin' to be better . . . do better. I've lived such an immoral and selfish life. You know how I won so much money from . . . We owned a convenience store gas station in the early days of Florida Lotto. Back when it wasn't as regulated as it is now. I was there all day every day scratching off tickets. Not buying them. I had no money. Just . . . taking them. I'd scratch them off until I'd find a winner, then I'd use part of the winnings to pay for all the scratch-offs I had gone through. I cheated. I'm a crook. I . . . did that for a while before anyone ever realized what I was doing. And then I didn't just do it in my name. I'd use my wife. My mom. Buddies I'd pay a fee for lettin' me use their name. But now, I just wanted to do something right for once, something good."

"But you can't," Blade says. "If you can't pay us for all we've done on the case already, then that's us doin' good, not you. Got nothin' to do with you."

"You wouldn't be doing it if I hadn't hired you to."

"But you didn't hire us," she says. "You tricked us. You want some karma credit for that?"

"What are you going to do?" he asks. "Please don't tell anyone. Please don't tell Heather."

"I wonder," Blade says. "Do you have any idea how much money has passed through your hands over the years. Any idea?"

"A . . . lot."

"And how much of that was spent on yourself?"

"Most of it."

"This whole time we could'a been doin' work we get paid for so, you know, we can go on living and not lose our agency or home or car. But you don't care, do you? Because once a selfish bastard asshole, always a selfish bastard asshole."

"I'm payin' for my transgressions—"

"Bitch, your broke ass ain't payin' for shit," she says. "That's the whole point. You dying. Well, guess what? We all do. Maybe your ass is dyin' a few years shy of the life expectancy for a white man in this white man's world, but only a few years."

"Okay," I say to Blade, trying to get her to back off.

"No," she says. "It's not okay. Bitch messed with my money. With my life, my livelihood. Didn't just steal from the State of Florida. He stole from me."

"What're you gonna do?" he says, looking from her to me, his eyes pleading. "You've got to find her."

"Let me tell you what I ain't gonna do," Blade says. "What I don't do. I don't work for free. My black ass ain't a slave. Understand?"

THIRTY-THREE

"What are we gonna do?" I ask.

"Move on to the next case," Blade says.

We are back in her car driving out of the cemetery.

"I can't just quit this one."

"There is no *this one*," she says. "Can't quit a job you don't have."

To our right, two men are loading a small orange tractor with a backhoe attachment onto a trailer hooked to a white flatbed work truck near a freshly dug grave.

I wonder if their business cards say Gravediggers.

"You know what I mean."

"I ain't workin' for free," she says. "I'm worth more than that. You don't know what it's like to be a slave."

I start to say *Neither do you*, but she holds up her hand.

"It's in my DNA," she says.

Maybe it is. Who am I to say it's not?

She pulls into traffic on Lisenby and heads toward 98.

"You're not gettin' paid to deal with Rush's stalker," I say.

"Bet I will eventually," she says. "Call it an investment."

"We wouldn't be doing it for Iversen—or even Malcolm and Heather. We'd be doing it for Leah."

"For how long?" she asks. "Until it's solved? What if it never is? The bills come every month. Nobody we owe gonna say, 'You good, don't worry about payin' me, just find that little girl.'"

"What if we work on this one when we can, in between paying gigs—like we do with Kaylee's."

"Look how that's going," she said. "You know these kinds of cases take every ounce of our attention, focus, and resources."

The longer we talk, the more aggressive her driving becomes.

"What if we—"

"Who you think held all this shit together when your ass went to prison?" she says.

I realize I haven't fully comprehended how my incarceration affected her. I left her alone and she had survived, but it couldn't have been easy.

"And who you think gonna handle all this shit when your ass goes back? 'Cause you act like you tryin' your best to do just that."

I start to say something, to defend myself, but stop.

"I can't afford to fuck around," she says. "I'm runnin' a business. Not a goddamn charity."

THIRTY-FOUR

Lev Sokolov is a meaty man with a deep tan in his seventies. His large head is bald and a thick gold rope chain circles his thick neck. He's naked except for blue swim trunks, and his hard bulging belly slopes down to hang over the white drawstring.

He's just stepped out of the bay onto the small sandy beach and is still wet, the beads of water shimmering on his dark skin.

"Swim every day," he says. "But I like it best when it's cold."

Across Beach Drive where his nephew had chased and shot at me the night before, his glass-front mansion refracts the midmorning sun.

Lev's bodyguard, who could be Bogdan but isn't, stands about ten feet away dressed in all black and wearing dark sunglasses.

"Thank you for agreeing to see me," I say.

He waves his hand. "I understand we have a mutual problem."

He speaks with nearly no discernible accent.

"I'm here in hopes we can find a peaceful resolution."

"I'm familiar with you and your partner," he says. "Almost hired you to find someone last year but . . . they turned up before we did."

Even beneath the midmorning sun the day is chilly, the breeze blowing in off the bay, cold, but Lev doesn't ask for a towel or clothes, just stands there drip-drying.

"I like what I've seen of your work," he says. "What I've read and heard, what our research turned up. I can see a day in the future where I will employ your services."

"And we'd still like to be here so you can."

He shakes his large head slowly, the gold chain glinting. "My sister's kid. Tryin' to bring him along, but . . . I have no sons of my own. Had hoped he'd . . . be someone to take over certain aspects of my businesses, but . . ."

I nod and listen.

"What did he do to you?"

"I was in your club a few nights ago, which I enjoyed as usual."

He nods. "Glad to hear it. It's a nice place, no?"

"It is. As I walked to my car, he approached me with Bogdan and said I owed him money for the young woman I was in VIP with."

"Owed *him* money?" he asks. "For *her*?"

I nod.

"You paid for the room and whatever the young woman charged you?"

"Yes, sir."

"He say why?"

"He said I had had sex with her."

"So he's a pimp now? In my club."

"Last night I was called to pick up a client from your club," I say. "A grieving father who lost his daughter and had too much to drink. As I was driving him home, Dimitri and Bogdan came up on us where my client was vomiting in a ditch in a neighborhood between here and the club and began shooting at us. They then chased us, firing at us—shot my car to shit— including down your street here. A deputy friend of mine met us up at the intersection and Dimitri turned down a side street and drove away. I didn't report him or . . . I just drove to where the deputy was sitting, hoping he'd stop pursuing us before someone got killed."

"I appreciate that," he says. "And I appreciate that your partner only injured and didn't kill them."

So he'd heard about that.

"I'm looking for a peaceful resolution," I say.

"I run legitimate businesses," he says. "Can't have this type of . . . But . . . I can't let anything happen to my sister's kid, you know?"

I nod.

"If something were to happen to him," he says, "I'd have to . . . respond to the person who . . . was responsible."

"I figured," I say. "And that's what I'm trying to prevent. If something happened to me or my partner . . . we have family and close friends—on both sides of the law—who would also have to respond. And I honestly don't know which one would be worse, but either side would dismantle everything piece by piece."

"I don't want a war," he says. "I'm too old. Have too much to lose. Want to finish my life with as little stress as possible."

"We want the same thing," I say. "I don't want to die. And you don't want to kill me."

"Thank you for coming to me with this with respect. I'll talk to Dimitri. We'll get this resolved."

THIRTY-FIVE

"I'm not sure I feel any safer," Lexi is saying.

"I'm not sure you should."

We are in my kitchen cooking dinner.

I still haven't heard from Blade. We haven't spoken since our conversation in the car about the case, though I've tried to reach her a few times.

"I still can't believe you met with him," she says. "'What did you do today?' 'Oh, not much. Just met with a mostly naked Russian mobster.'"

"It's all fun and games until someone gets his dick shot off."

"God, I hope that doesn't happen," she says. "Do you have any idea how much I love that particular part of your body?"

"I have some idea," I say. "Pretty damn fond of it myself."

"Please be extra careful," she says. "Especially if Blade's not gonna be around."

"She'll be around—or I'll be around her. I'm gonna work the next case with her. Just gonna keep workin' Leah's on my own as I can."

"I hate that you can't carry a weapon," she says.

"It's usually not an issue, but . . . until the Dimitri thing is resolved . . ."

"I'll hang around more if you'll have me."

"We're already taking more risks than we should."

"This is worth the risks," she says. "Obviously. And when it comes to keepin' you safe . . ."

"I could just get a weapon and hope I don't get caught. That way you wouldn't be at risk."

"I don't mind the risk," she says. "Hell, I'd . . . just go get another job if I weren't in the perfect position to help keep you from going back to prison. We've just got to make it two years."

"That seems like a very, very long time."

"We can do it. Just have to be careful and smart."

"You being here like this isn't smart. And what happens when Logan starts blackmailing you?"

Logan Owens doesn't just have evidence that would send me back to prison. He has evidence that would cause Lexi to lose her job and maybe even be brought up on criminal charges.

"'Cause you know he's going to eventually," I add.

"So many things could happen to him before then," she says. "Dimitri could take him off the board. Or he could get arrested and—"

"If he gets arrested, he'll trade what he has on you and me for a reduced sentence."

"You're probably right," she says.

We are quiet a moment, the ominousness of the situation hanging between us like a thick humidity in the air.

"I'd like to help you with Leah's case if I can," she says. "I've been reading a lot about it and I think I could . . . be of some use to you. And since you don't have Blade's help anymore . . ."

She tells me what she knows, and I fill in any gaps.

"So why would a little girl who's afraid of the dark and bad weather go out in a dark night in the middle of a hurricane?" she says.

"That is the question."

"I have two theories," she says.

"Lay 'em on me."

"The first . . . She was sleepwalking."

"Interesting," I say.

"You've already thought of it," she says. "So tell me why it couldn't be that."

"It's possible," I say. "It would explain what got her out of the condo at that time in those conditions, but it wouldn't keep her out. She would wake up eventually and come back."

"Unless someone snatched her or something happened to her once she was out there."

"True."

"But?"

"The packing and planning involved makes me think she wasn't sleepwalking," I say. "I also think the rain would've caused her to wake up pretty quickly. And the fact that she ran from Ethan Storm—"

"Who?"

"The storm chaser who saw her at Thomas and Front Beach and tried to help her."

She nods. "Okay. Second theory. I don't think she ran away."

"What do you mean?"

"I don't think she decided to run away and then did it. I think she had an appointment, was meeting someone, so had to go when she did. If she was just running away, I think she would've waited until a better time—like when it wasn't storming."

I nod. "I agree," I say. "Given her fears and the circumstances, there had to be a powerful motivating factor to get her out of that condo—whether pushing her from within or pulling her from without."

"And think about what she packed," she says. "Or what she didn't pack. She took clothes—a few changes of clothes. She took a book and a few entertainment and comfort items, but she didn't take any food or water. It's like she knew the place she was going would have those things. She didn't think she'd be on her own trying to survive as in a runaway situation."

"That's good."

"I know I'm not offering anything you haven't thought of, but . . . can I keep going?"

"Please. And that last one was something I hadn't thought of."

"The picture in her backpack," she says. "I think that's the key. I think either she was going to meet that little girl or help her or something like that. I think it's entirely possible that a predator was using the pic to lure her out. That's why no one was ever able to identify her."

"I certainly think that's possible," I say. "But I haven't been able to find out how or when a predator would've been able to engage with her. This was before social media. She didn't have a phone. I agree it's a likely scenario. I'd just like to find out how it was done."

"Could've just been a pen pal situation," she says. "She thought she was writing to the little girl in the photo, but it was really some creep all along."

I nod.

"What about the book?" she asks. "Any clues there?"

"Not that I can figure out. It was a school library edition of *The Secret Garden*."

"I read that as a girl," she says. "It's a great book. Magical."

"They were reading *The Whipping Boy* at school," I say.

"And some people theorize that has something to do with her running away because the main characters in it run away."

"I haven't heard of it," she says, pulling it up on her phone and reading the description. "'Prince Brat and his whipping boy inadvertently trade places after becoming involved with dangerous outlaws. The two boys have nothing in common and even less reason to like each other. But when they find themselves taken hostage after running away, they are left with no choice but to trust each other.'"

"I think it's a stretch," I say. "And you have to believe she actually ran away for it to fit, but plenty of internet sleuths are convinced."

"I still say if she was going to run away, she'd've waited for a better time to do it."

"Yeah. And there's just nothing we've found to suggest she had a reason to run away. Statistically, she was a little too young to be a runaway."

"I don't feel like I'm being helpful," she says.

"It's not you. It's this case. I don't feel like I'm any closer to finding out what happened to her than I was when I started. And I'm not sure I ever will be. Maybe Blade is right. Maybe I should let it go and move on."

"Do you think you can?"

THIRTY-SIX

"Hey Luc," Arthur is saying. "Hey Luc. Look at this. Look at this. You ever seen one of these?"

Arthur Whitten-Collins is a large, overweight man with thick dark wavy hair, and though he's pushing forty he acts four.

We are in his mother's storage shed and he's showing me some of his old toys—rummaging around through old boxes, going from toy to toy.

Blade wasn't in the office this morning and is still not answering my texts.

"Hey, Luc. Hey, Luc. You ever seen one of these?"

He holds up a plastic space laser.

"It's a . . . it's a . . . Supersonic Blaster 2000. Cool, isn't it?"

I hold up a picture of Leah—one of the last ever taken of her. "Hey, Arthur," I say. "Do you know who this is?"

"She's . . . That's my friend. She's my friend. Her name is Leah. Leah's gone-gone. Leah went bye-bye."

"Do you know where she went?" I ask.

Marjorie says, "Arthur, where did Leah go?"

"Bye-bye. Leah went bye-bye. She's gone-gone."

"Who'd she go with?" I ask.

He doesn't respond.

"Who did Leah play with?" I ask.

"Leah played with Arthur," he says.

"Who else?" I ask. "Who else played with Leah and Arthur?"

"Kyle. Sadie. Brian. Steve."

I look at Marjorie.

"Leah's brother and best friend," she says. "And two boys from the neighborhood—one from here and one from the Flamingo. Neither of them lived here very long."

"No one plays with Arthur anymore," Arthur says. "Hey, Luc. Hey, Luc. You wanna play with me?"

"Yes, I do," I say.

He pulls out more toys and we begin playing.

"I miss playin' in here," he says.

Marjorie says, "I haven't let him play in here since . . . that night. Didn't feel right."

"This is my fort," he says. "I miss my fort."

"What did you play in your fort?"

"Toys," he says.

"Did Leah or anyone ever come in your fort without you?" I ask.

"It's Arthur's fort."

"They didn't come in without you?" I ask.

"No way."

Marjorie makes eye contact with me. "He wouldn't know if they did. But I never saw any evidence until that night."

"Arthur," I say, "will you look at this picture and tell me whose toys these are?"

I take out a photo of the items Leah left in here the night she disappeared and hold it up for him to look at.

"Leah's," he says. "Those are Leah's. She gave them to me."

"She gave them to you?" I ask.

"Yeah. Well, some. Wouldn't let me have the . . . pet. I miss Leah. She was sweet to me. Where did she go? Can she come play?"

"When did she give them to you?"

"Yesterday," he says.

Marjorie says, "Anything that happened before the current moment is yesterday for him."

"I set them up to come play with my friends and then the storm took them away," he says.

"Leah gave them to you and then you set everything up so y'all could play with them the next time you played?" Marjorie asks.

"Yes, ma'am. And then they were gone," he says. "Bad storm. Blow them away. Like Leah. And Arthur can't play in fort anymore."

"If she gave them to him in the days before the storm . . ." Marjorie says.

"It would explain why they were identified as hers and would have her fingerprints on them. And it would mean she might not have stopped in here the night she disappeared."

THIRTY-SEVEN

"What're you sayin'?" Heather asks.

"That it's possible Leah wasn't in Marjorie Whitten-Collins's storage unit that night," I say.

Once again, I've found her on the balcony of her uncle's condo.

"Can't be absolutely certain," I say. "Arthur's not the most reliable witness I've ever dealt with, but . . . it seems as though it's at least possible."

"What does it mean?" she asks. "If it's true."

"It may mean nothing," I say. "It may not change anything. But we want to get the most accurate timeline we can. We don't want to believe she was somewhere she wasn't. It would mean that she didn't take the things found in there with her when she left that night. It would mean Marjorie and Arthur aren't suspects like I thought they were."

"Which is why they would say it," she says.

"Yeah, but Arthur doesn't seem capable of that kind of deception, and not only did Marjorie not coach him, she seemed genuinely surprised by what he said."

"Okay," she says, nodding. "You were there. I wasn't. I'm just suspicious of everyone. Have been for over twenty years now."

"The other thing it would mean . . ." I say. "If it's true . . . she would've had more time to get to the two places she was seen. It'd make it more likely that she could get down in front of the super clubs where Dixie Lee Jennings saw her and back to the intersection of Thomas and Front Beach where Ethan Storm saw her."

"I still . . . find it hard to believe she . . . was able to . . . in that storm, but . . . I find all of it hard to even imagine."

"I know. I'm so sorry. Loved ones just . . . vanishing . . . just gone . . . without any explanation is the most . . . difficult . . . kind of . . . limbo to be in."

She nods. "Your sister," she says. "You . . . get it. Most people don't."

"It's not the same," I say. "Can't compare to your child, to a young child at that, but . . . I can at least . . . relate in some small way."

She looks at me, our eyes locking, tears welling up in hers. She starts to say something but stops, and we sit in silence for a long moment.

Eventually, once the moment is past, I say, "Can you tell me anything about Brian or Steve?"

"Who?"

"Brian Meeks or Steve Saddler."

She shakes her head. "Who are they?"

"According to Arthur, kids that played with them."

"I thought I knew all of Leah's little friends."

"I'll ask Sadie if she remembers them," I say. "One of them lived down by Marjorie and Arthur and I was told the other boy lived here. In fact, I'll go see if I can find out more about them now."

I stand.

Unlike the other times I've been here, she stands too.

"How long has it been since you've eaten anything?" I ask. "Could I get you something before I go?"

She shakes her head. "I'm not hungry but thank you."

When I open the sliding glass door and step inside the condo, she follows me.

As I continue across the small living room to the little hallway near the front door, she continues with me as if walking me out.

At the door, I pause and say, "I'll be in touch. Will let you know as soon as I know anything."

I haven't mentioned Iversen's check bouncing or Blade quitting the case and I'm not going to—at least not until I have to.

She reaches up and embraces me.

I hug her back.

As I release her, she leans in and kisses me. It's a hard, awkward, painful kiss, and my lip feels like it's bleeding.

I'm stunned, not sure what to do.

She seems so fragile, so broken, I don't want to risk doing anything to hurt or break her further.

She pulls at my shirt but isn't tall enough to pull it over my head.

I'm not sure what to do, but I bend down so she can take it off.

As soon as she has it off, she takes off her dress, revealing her small, emaciated body. She's not wearing a bra or panties.

She then unbuttons my pants and pulls them and my underwear down to below my knees.

Kneeling on the hard tile floor, she takes me in her mouth.

And though I'm completely passive and don't really want

this to be happening, my body responds to hers and what she's doing.

After she has achieved her desired goal, she pulls me down and has me lie flat on the cold tile floor.

When I'm in a prone position, she straddles me, grabbing me hard and putting me inside her.

At first she moans and writhes and acts like a woman who hasn't had a man inside her in over twenty years, but soon she is sobbing.

She continues to move about and thrust as she cries, but her movements are slower now, seemingly more therapeutic than sexual.

I lie perfectly still except for reaching up and slowly and tenderly caressing her legs and arms.

I can't tell for sure if she came or not but she certainly reached a release.

Eventually, she falls onto me, her small bare breasts on my shirtless chest, and I hold her as she weeps.

She's so small and light on top of me as to almost not be there, but her small sobs send tremors down the length of my body.

"Thank you," she whispers. "Sorry about that. I . . . don't know what came over me."

"Are you okay?" I ask.

"No," she says, "but I'm better than I've been in a long, long time. I'm sure I'll feel embarrassed soon and be filled with regret, but right now . . . I feel as if I'm actually alive and in some way connected to another living human being."

"Please don't ever feel embarrassed or have any regret," I say. "Just focus on the life and the connection . . . to life and . . . humanity."

"I think I just might," she says. "Do you want to . . ."

I'm still inside her.

"Do you to . . . finish?" she asks. "I feel like I've just used you. It wouldn't be fair to leave you frustrated or—"

"I'm in no way frustrated," I say, and hold her tighter. "There's only one thing I want. I want you to not even think about this again. I want you to let it be what it was, take any . . . good thing you can from it . . . and nothing else."

"I'll try," she says, "but I have a tendency to overthink and fixate."

"I figured. And I don't want you to feel guilty. I don't mean about me or even Malcolm. I mean about Leah. This wasn't a betrayal of her in any way. Your grief's gonna try to use guilt to—"

She begins sobbing again, this time deep, wrenching spasms that rock her entire body—and maybe even her being—and as she weeps, I hold her tightly against me, trying to absorb some of her loss.

THIRTY-EIGHT

I find Sadie Arnold and her dermatologist dad having lunch together at Panaroma pizza on 23rd Street.

They are both in scrubs, and though she's in her early thirties and he's in his fifties, with his trim physique, dyed hair and beard, and the work he'd had done on his face, they look like they could be a couple instead of father and daughter. Except for their eyes. Their eyes give them away. They both have the same almond-shaped brown eyes.

When I was a kid, Panaroma Pizza was in the Panama City Mall food court, and I used to eat there regularly. It was across from the movie theater, and I'd often grab a slice before or after catching a flick. Now the mall is no more. It was on life-support for a while, but Hurricane Michael finally pulled the plug.

Erik and Sadie are polite in a formal sort of way with one another, but there's no real warmth between them.

Erik says, "We have a daddy daughter lunch date every Wednesday and go to a different place each time. Been doing it a while and haven't repeated a place yet."

"I appreciate y'all letting me intrude," I say. "I'll be quick."

I quickly tell them about the things that were found in the storage unit and what Arthur told me.

Sadie says, "She was very generous. Always giving her stuff away. I could see her giving Arthur most of those things. But not the Giga Pet. She didn't trust him with that."

Erik says, "You know how kids that aren't taken care of very well don't take care of themselves or their stuff? She was like that. She'd leave her toys and things at my condo all the time. I already told you she had no boundaries. She also didn't take care of things either."

"You never liked her," Sadie says. "What I call fun and free, you call having no boundaries. What I call generous, you call not taking care of things."

"It wasn't that I didn't like her per se," he says. "She was just . . . a little heathen. Wild—like she had been raised by wolves. I'm not surprised something happened to her—given how little supervision she had and what a wild child she was."

"I thought she was so cool," Sadie says. "I wanted to be like her. More . . . fun and carefree. I'd wake up in the morning and she'd be in the bed with me. She hadn't been when I went to bed. I'd be sitting watching TV and look away when a commercial came on, and she'd be sitting on the couch watching it with me. She was always on an adventure, always pretending and imagining. She was a part of the most magical moments of my childhood."

"How about Brian and Steve?" I ask. "What can you tell me about them?"

"I don't remember a Steve," she says. "But Brian was this sort of sad kid who lived in one of the townhomes near Arthur. He'd play with us sometimes. Sadie was really sweet to him, always tryin' to cheer him up."

"Did they like each other?" I ask. "Were they like boyfriend and girlfriend or anything?"

She shrugs and shakes her head, her ponytail whipping from side to side. "Maybe. I've really never thought of them in that way, but . . . maybe, I guess. They were definitely buddies. She was . . . nicer to him than anyone else was."

I look at Erik. "And you don't remember a Steve?"

He shakes his head. "I don't remember either of them. But we never had a lot of kids over. Wouldn't've had Leah over as much as we did if she hadn't just kept showing up."

Brian Meeks works for UPS. He drives one of the iconic brown trucks delivering packages, mostly from Amazon these days, to people in the east end of Panama City.

I find him parked in the large empty parking lot of an abandoned shopping center off Tyndall Parkway in Callaway eating a packed lunch. What's left of the supermarket, the Chinese Buffet, the plus-size women's clothing store, the hair and nail salon, and the department store looks as if it has been bombed, but its fatal wounds were inflicted by Hurricane Michael.

"I'm still messed up about that," he says. "Guess I always will be. To be a small kid like that and actually know a kid who goes missing . . . It gets in your head. Not that my head was a good place before it happened."

He's sitting in the driver's seat eating a crustless sandwich like a kid, taking small bites and chewing slowly between talking. I'm standing down on the ground near the open right-side door.

He shakes his head and gets a far-off look as he seems to be thinking back to that time.

"It was such a strange thing to have happen. Scarred me, you know? A few years later, I saw her picture on a milk cartoon. Freaked me out more than I can tell you."

"What can you tell me about Arthur?"

"He was a sweetheart. Just a big kid. Like our own gentle giant. He was so much bigger than the rest of us but acted so much younger."

"And the fort in his mom's storage unit?"

"Just a positive place for us to go, get away from all that bad shit in our lives. Wasn't much to it. It was kind of boring, but nothing bad ever happened there."

"Who all played there?"

"Arthur, me, Kyle, Sadie, Leah . . . We were the regulars. I guess from time to time there were other kids, but they were just sort of random—brought by one of the others."

"What about Steve?"

"Steve?"

"Do you remember a Steve playing with y'all?"

He shakes his head. "I don't . . . I can't remember a kid by that name. I don't know."

"How close were you to Leah?" I ask. "Was she your girl-friend or—"

"I wanted her to be. I did not have a good childhood. My parents fought all the time. I . . . I realize now that I was depressed and needed medication and counseling, but back then . . . I just knew I was unhappy. And the only . . . and I mean the *only* bright spot was Leah. She was the most happy person I ever knew. Had the most energy. Was always playing and playful. Pretending. Making up games and adventures. She could make anything fun. There hasn't been a single day I haven't thought about her or missed her or wish things could've been different since it happened."

"What do you think happened?"

"I . . . I feel so . . . I haven't told anyone this since the first and only police officer I spoke to back then, but I think . . . she was coming to get me. I feel . . . guilty. I was . . . I hated my life. I was so miserable. I was always talkin' about running away, disappearing so no one could find me. I think I said something about the storm carrying me away and never being seen again. I was just a stupid, depressed kid, but I've always wondered if anything I said caused her to do what she did. I think it did. I think she was coming to run away with me."

"Did you see her that night?"

"No."

"Did anything happen to make you think she had come to your house during the storm?"

"Just her breaking into our fort and waiting for me there. I don't know if she tried to get into my house and couldn't or just thought I'd meet her there, but . . ."

"We think it might be possible that she gave the items found there to Arthur before that night and he left them there," I say. "She may not have even gone over there that night."

"Really?"

I nod and tell him what was found in the storage unit.

He shakes his head. "She was always giving things away. We all sort of traded things back and forth, but she would give her stuff and not expect anything in return. But . . . I don't think she'd give a Giga Pet to Arthur because he'd kill it. He didn't have the . . . capacity to care for them. The ones his mother got him he always . . . He never took care of them and it bothered Leah. With her imagination . . . She always acted as if they were real. Like she really believed it. She was always taking care of everyone—like a little mama—especially her brother, and she was that way over those silly pets too. I never saw her give one to Arthur. And I remember her tellin' him *no* when he asked her for hers."

FORTY

Back in the car I try Blade again.

She still hasn't responded to my texts—and my phone shows they've been delivered but not read.

All my calls go straight to voicemail.

I open my Find My app and search her location.

Her location is no longer listed.

She hadn't stopped sharing her location with me. If she had, I would've received a notification, so either she turned all her Location Services off or her phone itself is off.

Now I'm worried.

Before I thought she was ignoring me because she was still pissed at me, but now it seems like something different all together.

I swipe Find My closed and call Pete.

"You heard anything from Blade?" I ask.

"Not in a few days. Why?"

I tell him.

"Sounds like her phone is off," he says. "Would also explain the texts not being read and the calls going straight to voice-mail. When's the last time you saw her?"

"Yesterday morning," I say. "We had just met with Richard Iversen. His check bounced and she wanted to quit the case and I didn't. We argued a little about it, but it was no big deal."

"We need to see if anyone else has heard from her," he says. "You check with Ashlynn and Ben. I'll make some calls. See if I can track her phone."

"Okay. Thanks."

"You think this could be related to the case?" he asks.

"It's possible, I guess, but . . . I think it's more likely it's Dimitri."

FORTY-ONE

When Malcolm and Heather ask to meet with me at their old condo the next morning, I wonder if it has anything to do with what happened between Heather and me the day before.

I find them inside the condo, sitting in the living room. Kyle is with them. It's the first time I've ever seen the three of them together.

Everyone acts like they have the other times I've been with them. I don't sense any underlying tension or weirdness, and Heather doesn't give any indication that we've ever had private conversations let alone that I've been inside her.

Malcolm says, "Thanks for coming. We appreciate it."

"No problem," I say. "What's up?"

"Richard told us what happened," he says.

I assume he's talking about Richard Iversen's check bouncing, but I ask because I've learned not to assume.

"That he hasn't paid y'all and can't," he says.

"Oh that," I say.

"We had no idea he was . . . broke," Heather says.

"I don't think he did either," I say.

"He's very sick," Malcolm says. "Doesn't have long."

Heather adds, "Easy for details to get lost."

I nod.

"We were shocked when he said he wanted to hire someone to see if we could find Leah and finally figure out what happened," Heather says. "We haven't had any contact with him over the years. Didn't know anything about him. It was such an odd and grandiose thing to do. But we didn't feel like we could refuse the help. We knew he was wealthy—or had been. We just took him at his word that he could afford to pay for the investigation."

"We did too," I say.

"But . . ." Heather says, "you've continued . . . to work on the case even after he told you he couldn't pay you."

I nod again. "I couldn't just stop."

"Were you going to tell us?" she asks.

"Probably at some point," I say. "Wasn't in a hurry to add something like this to your grief and—"

"We appreciate that," Malcolm says. "But we'd like to talk to you about what we can do moving forward and—"

"What about your partner?" Heather asks. "You said you couldn't just stop the case. What about her?"

"She might have to work a paying case while I do this one or we may both do some of both. We'll have to figure that out."

"We really don't want y'all to quit," Malcolm says. "We can't pay you what Richard was, but I'm sure we can come up with something. I'm willing to spend every dime I have or can make on finding her. That's what people don't understand. I love both our children and would do anything I could for them. I've never seen Leah as a stepdaughter, just a daughter."

Kyle nods, then looks at Heather. "It's true. You've never believed it but it's true."

She doesn't respond.

"I know Heather loves Kyle like her own and I always loved Leah like my own. We've always taken good care of each other in this family and always will—or the best we can under the circumstances."

Heather nods and gives him a smile of acknowledgement.

"I've got a few thousand put up for an emergency that may arrive. It's all yours. Please just find her."

Kyle looks at me. "Are you making any progress? Should we keep going or are we just wasting our money and time?"

"So far it's only *our* time and money," I say, "and I don't see it as wasted at all."

"Can you share anything with us?" Malcolm says.

"We think it's at least possible she didn't break into Marjorie Whitten-Collins's storage unit that night."

"Really?" Malcolm says. "Why?"

I tell them.

"So what?" Kyle says. "What does that matter? Is that all you've got?"

"It matters because our best chance of finding out what happened to her that night is to know exactly what she did and when."

"Okay, but that's not much to have for . . . And doesn't narrow it down much at all, does it? Besides . . . I agree with Sadie and Brian. Leah wouldn't give her Giga Pet to Arthur. She treated them like they were real. So maybe she did go in there that night after all. And if that's true then you have nothing."

"What can you tell me about Brian?" I ask.

"Brian who?"

"Meeks."

"He was a kid who played with us some back then," he says. "Was more of a friend of Arthur's than ours. Why?"

"He talked to Leah or at least in front of her about running away on the night of the storm and he thinks she may have been coming to help him or stop him or something."

"Oh wow," Kyle says. "That . . . that makes a certain sense, I guess."

"It's just the sort of thing she'd do," Heather says. "Have an adventure and save someone."

Malcolm says, "It would explain what got her out in that storm."

"Did he see her that night?" Kyle asks.

"Says he didn't."

"See?" Malcolm says, speaking more to Kyle than anyone else. "This is progress. We can't stop now. We have to keep going."

"Thinking back now in the light of this . . ." I say. "Do you remember Leah saying anything about Brian or him being sad or wanting to run away or . . ."

Kyle says, "Maybe she did say something about him. Can't remember what exactly. I was . . . I only half-listened to her."

Malcolm looks at me. "This is good. Things are happening. Are you willing to keep going if we can pay you . . . something?"

Heather says, "He was willing to when he wasn't getting paid anything at all."

"I don't want to take your emergency savings," I say. "Let me keep doing what I'm doing for as long as I can. I'll let you know if I have to stop or if an expense comes up that I need help with."

WHEN MALCOLM and Kyle are gone, Heather and I step out onto the balcony.

"You don't have to be afraid to be alone with me," she says. "I'm not gonna jump you again. I promise. I feel so . . . embarrassed."

"You have nothing to be embarrassed about."

"I wanted to apologize to you and to thank you for being so . . . sweet. And for how you're acting now. It shows a level of kindness that is . . . rare. I wanted to say I'm sorry and it won't happen again, but I also wanted you to know that it was . . . very healing. I know it had to be cringeworthy for you—a depressed woman twice your age humping you like a . . . But for me it was . . . It . . . It reached something inside me I thought was not just dormant but dead."

"You have nothing to apologize for," I say. "Nothing to feel embarrassed about. I'm . . . honored to have been a small part of it."

"You're so gentle and sweet," she says. "Thank you. I can't see you going to prison for battery. Don't detect any brutality or rage in you at all."

"It's there," I say. "I do my best to keep the beast in the cage, but it gets out sometimes."

"Human beings are endlessly interesting creatures," she says. "Some of them anyway. I can't believe you're working our case for free."

We are quiet a moment.

"Why were Malcolm and Kyle saying the things about family and—"

"Very, very early on I said something about he'd be doing more if it were Kyle missing, that he'd act differently if Leah were his. I was out of my mind with grief and . . . He can't let it go. And evidently he said something to Kyle about it at some point. We got together when the kids were still young and they are like our own in many ways, but . . . the step thing comes up occasionally. How could it not? But when something happens like did to Leah . . . it causes a sort of fault line. I don't know. I wish I had never said anything back then. I wish he'd let it go, see it for what it was, but . . . I guess that's not going to happen. And I guess I really don't care."

FORTY-TWO

"Anything?" Pete is asking

I know he's referring to Blade, asking if I've heard anything or come up with anything on her whereabouts.

"Nothing," I say. "You?"

"Striking out everywhere," he says. "Nobody's seen or heard anything."

"I've got a meeting with Clyde Broussard this afternoon," I say. "Gonna see if Logan has anything to do with it or knows anything about it. Then I'm gonna talk to Rush."

"Who?"

"Cindi Rush," I say. "Someone Blade's interested in. Was gonna help her with an ex who was stalking her. If there's nothing with either of them . . . I'll go to Dimitri or at least Lev."

"Let me know if you need backup or what else I can do to help," he says.

"Thanks. But I'll try to keep you away from the criminal element."

"I tried to have her phone tracked," he says. "It's definitely off. Not pinging on any towers. Can't trace it. Can't triangulate a location if it doesn't ping off any towers."

"Something's wrong," I say. "Bad wrong."

"I'm afraid so too," he says.

We fall silent a moment.

Eventually, he says, "I'll keep trying. Hopefully you'll turn up something this afternoon. We won't stop until we find her."

"Thanks," I say. "And thanks for all your help."

"Of course," he says. "Not as close as y'all, but . . . she's my sister too."

"I know."

"Got something for you on your case too," he says. "Not sure if you want it, but—"

"Definitely," I say. "Not stopping."

"Spoke to Iversen's accountant and bank," he says. "He's been broke a while and he knew about it. It didn't come as a surprise to him like he pretended. He knew the check he wrote you was bad when he wrote it."

FORTY-THREE

"Why hire us?" I ask.

"Huh?" he asks, looking up at me.

"Why do any of this? Why knowingly write us a bad check?"

"I just want that little girl found," he says.

"Why?"

"What do you mean? Who wouldn't?"

"Who would use a bad check to hire a firm to find her?"

"I should've done it a long time ago—back when I still had my money, but I didn't. So . . . I'm trying to . . ."

"Make up for being selfish? A cheat and a thief? What?"

"I'm not trying to buy my way into heaven," he says.

"Good, 'cause you're out of money."

"But I am trying to do some good, set some things right before I make the transition."

"But of all the things you could do," I say, "why this one?"

"What do you mean?"

"You could be trying to do good in a lot of different ways. Why this one? Why such special interest in this one? What do you feel so guilty about? Was it something you did to her before her disappearance or did you have something to do with her disappearance?"

"Neither," he says. "My God. I'm sorry the check didn't clear, but that's no reason to come harass a dying man."

"This isn't about the money," I say. "I don't care about the money. I want to know why you're—"

I stop and turn as something occurs to me.

Scanning across the cemetery, I look beyond the traffic on Lisenby to the place across the street where Leah's backpack had been buried.

"Why bury her backpack over there?" I ask.

"Huh?"

"Her backpack. Why'd you bury it over there?"

"I didn't. I didn't do anything with her backpack or anything else."

I look back at the grave. "Your wife's funeral was . . . two days after Leah went missing."

"Yeah. Why?"

"Which means it was an open grave the night Leah disappeared. Did you bury her in there? Is she under your wife's coffin?"

"What the— Get the hell away from here. Now. How dare you? This is sacred ground. This is my wife's . . . Have you no shame? I had nothing to do with that little girl's death and I sure wouldn't defile my wife's grave by putting her body in it. I'm glad my check bounced. I should've never hired you. You're crazy. And sick. And . . ."

He pitches forward onto the ground.

FORTY-FOUR

"You want to do *what?*" Pete asks.

I've just told him I'd like to look under Jane Iversen's grave.

He's standing with me near the spot where Richard Iversen collapsed a short while before.

After Iversen fell to the ground, I checked to see if he was faking, merely attempting to avoid my questions. When it seemed as though his acute distress was legit, I had called for emergency services. He's now on the way to the hospital with instructions for Pete to be notified if his condition changes.

"Is that what you were tellin' Iversen when he keeled over?"

"No," I say. "I hadn't gotten to that part yet. I was accusing him of murdering Leah and placing her body in the open grave the night before his wife's burial."

"Oh, good," he said. "For a minute there I thought you had done something to induce heart failure in a sick old man."

"Think about it, Pete," I say. "Why would her backpack be found over there?"

I point to the spot across Lisenby where the Unity church used to be and where Leah's backpack was found.

"Why is right. Why keep it at all? Why not destroy it? Why put it in trash bags before burying it? To preserve it. But why preserve it?"

"To revisit it," I say. "He wanted a trophy, wanted things of her, but he was smart enough not to keep them at his condo. So . . . he's out here burying her body in his wife's open grave that was already six feet deep—all he had to do was dig a little deeper and place Leah's body in it and the next day it'd be covered up with a coffin, six feet of dirt, and a granite grave marker—and he looks around and decides to bury her backpack over there."

"It's actually a good idea or theory or whatever, but that's all it is," he says. "You have no evidence. None at all."

"Why did he hire us?" I ask. "Why does he feel so guilty?"

"Good questions," he says. "Really. You should try to find the answers."

"What if the answer is under this grave?"

"You're not going to get permission to dig that grave up without some damn good and persuasive evidence. And you know that."

I nod and let out a long, heavy sigh. "I do."

"And if you do it yourself—or disturb the grave in any way, it's a felony. You'll go back to prison for a lot longer than two more years."

"I know."

"It's a good theory," he says. "But . . . that's all it is. There are a lot of good and interesting theories in this case. The internet is full of them. Just like in Kaylee's case. What if some armchair detectives showed up at your place tonight and said they believed Kaylee's body was buried under the foundation of your apartment and they wanted to jackhammer your floor and dig down under your foundation?"

"It's a little different—"

"Not much."

"—but I get your point."

"Let's look at Iversen harder," he says. "See if there's any evidence that he had anything to do with Leah's disappearance. If there's any evidence at all, it'll make your theory far more convincing and we might just be able to take a look under there."

FORTY-FIVE

"Blade's missing," I say.

"Since when?" Clyde asks.

"Last two days," I say.

We're on the small asphalt driveway at the opposite end of the cemetery, inside our vehicles that are facing opposite directions with our windows rolled down.

The huge black SUV he's in gleams in the sun, its buffed and polished clear coat like a mirror for my small bullet-riddled car.

"Wanted to make sure Logan didn't have anything to do with it before I go knocking on other doors," I say.

His vehicle is so much bigger than mine I have to crane my neck to look up at him.

He shakes his enormous head. "He got nothin' to do with it."

"Figured," I say. "Just wanted to make sure."

He shifts the weight of his mammoth frame and the leather seat squeaks and the entire vehicle moves as the springs and shocks on this side absorb the energy.

"We been in Orlando a couple of days. Just got back last night."

"And you haven't heard anything?"

"Would've told you."

"I figured," I say. "I meant now that you know she's missing have you heard anything that might be related."

He shakes his head.

"I'm thinking it's Dimitri," I say, "but . . . it could have something to do with a case we're working or one we've worked in the past."

"Y'all around more criminals than I am."

"Ain't that the damn truth," I say.

"Sorry to hear about Blade," he says. "I'll see what I can do to help find her."

"Anything happening between Logan and Dimitri?" I ask.

"Not really. Not yet. Logan's asking around about him, but that's about it."

"Not anxious to take on the Russian mob?"

He shrugs. "That's what you 'bout to do, ain't it?"

"If they have Blade."

"Holla if you need help."

FORTY-SIX

When I walk into Tootsie's and find someone else playing though Rush is on the schedule, I ask the bartender about it.

She's a tall, thin blond with a Nordic nose and a slightly nasally voice.

"Hasn't shown up at all this week," she says. "Not like her. Hasn't called or anything. She's burning bridges on some good gigs."

"May be out of her control," I say.

"Let's hope so. I like her."

I order a drink, pull out my phone, and begin to search through Rush's social media.

Her relationship status on Facebook says Complicated, and though she's not officially in a relationship with anyone, it's obvious from the pictures and posts that she's seeing a young woman named Blakely Mann.

Going further back in her history, I search for exes who could be the potential stalker.

It takes a while, but eventually I find a young woman who's in several pictures but whose name isn't a live link any longer.

Her name is Chrissy Violet and many of the pictures of the two of them show intimacy, but just as many appear to depict erratic behavior, excessive drinking, tears, anger, rage, and general volatility.

I step outside Tootsie's and call Blakely Mann through the Facebook app.

I don't expect her to answer but to my surprise she does.

I tell her who I am and explain why I'm calling.

"I haven't seen or heard from her in two days," she says. "I'm . . . This isn't like her. I didn't know what to do. I don't want to be stalkerish or anything, but . . . if I still hadn't heard anything by tomorrow, I was going to call the police."

"Any ideas where she might be?"

"No."

"She ever done anything like this before?"

"No."

"She told us she had been stalked and harassed," I say.

"Yeah. Her ex is a psycho cunt from hell."

"What's her name?"

"Chrissy," she says. "Chrissy Violet."

"Think she could have anything to do with—"

"Cindi would never go back to her," she says. "Never. Not in this lifetime."

"I didn't mean willingly," I say.

"Huh?"

"Do you think Chrissy could've . . . abducted her or—"

"She's crazy enough, but she's not big and strong enough. Cindi is small but she's tough and scrappy. Chrissy's even smaller than Cindi."

"Maybe she has help," I say.

"I doubt it. No way she has, like, actual friends. She probably just has, like, crazy person power."

FORTY-SEVEN

"Hey stranger," Lexi says.

I'm in my car in the parking lot of the Sunset Plaza shopping center staking out Chrissy Violet when she calls.

Violet works in a sex shop called Adam's Eve.

"Hey."

Sunset Plaza on Front Beach Road is one of the oldest strip malls in Panama City Beach and it looks like it. Mom-and-pop shops fill the small streaked-glass storefronts beneath a weathered and rusted tin roof. The asphalt parking lot is oil stained and potholed, and the random planted palms are leaning and look hurricane beaten.

"Are you avoiding me?"

The truth is I have been—since what happened with Heather Harrison. Even though I feel like it was something that was done to me more than something I did, I not only didn't stop it, I participated in it. I don't feel guilty exactly. Well, I guess I do. Some. But I just felt like I needed some space—time to decide if I'm going to tell her or not.

"No," I lie. "Of course not. Been busy with the case and . . . Blade."

"She still missing?"

"Yeah."

"Any idea where she might be?"

"Maybe," I say. "Friend of mine she was interested in and helping with a stalker is missing too, so . . ."

"You think they ran away together?"

I laugh. "It's funny. That hadn't actually crossed my mind."

"What then?"

"If just Blade was missing, I'd suspect Dimitri or someone else from another case we've worked—maybe even the one we're working now, but with Rush missing too, I think it's likely it's Rush's stalker."

"Do you know who she is and where she might have them?"

"Think so," I say. "I'm following her, hoping she'll lead me to them. She works at Adam's Eve. I'm in the parking lot waiting for her to get off."

"Shouldn't take long in Adam's Eve," she says. "Want some company?"

I really don't, but I say, "Sure."

According to Adam's Eve's website, it's a place where all your dreams related to sexual health, wellness, and pleasure come true. Adam's Eve believes that everyone deserves sexual pleasure, so whether you're looking for sex toys for women, sex toys for men, or sex toys for couples, they have adult toys for any rendezvous. Ready to take your sexual pleasure to the next level? Adam's Eve is your one-stop shop to help you reach orgasm and fulfill all your wildest fantasies.

As I wait for Chrissy to get off work and Lexi to arrive, I occupy myself by thinking through the case, trying my best to question every assumption, examine every detail, recall every witness statement. Jumbling up the various bits of information, tossing around the few facts, I attempt to place them beside each other in a variety of different ways to see if the new juxtapositions reveal any additional insights.

Why did Leah leave that night? Why did she take the things she did? Why break into Marjorie's storage unit? Why leave things there? Why did she go in two different directions on Thomas Drive, or did she? Who is the little girl in the school picture in her backpack?

Later, when Lexi slips into the passenger side, I say, "Are you ready to take your sexual pleasure to the next level?"

"Always," she says.

"You've come to the right place."

"I bet I have," she says, her eyes lingering lasciviously on me, though I had nodded at the sex shop. "I've missed you."

She leans over and gives me a long, deep, lingering kiss.

"Bet that's better than anything they have in there," I say.

I'm happy to see her and realize it was a mistake to avoid her.

"That's sweet," she says. "I wasn't sure you liked me anymore."

"I definitely do," I say. "Sorry I've been so . . . distracted with this case and Blade."

"That's to be expected," she says. "I thought it was more than that."

"It is," I say. "Or was."

"What is it?" she asks.

"My own stupidity," I say. "I've been way too in my head and . . . it's been firmly up my ass. I'm very sorry."

"Don't be. I'm just glad that's all it is."

I smile at her and caress her cheek with the back of my hand.

"I know what we've got is complicated and challenging,"

she says. "But it's pretty damn rare too. I'd hate to see us give up on it before we really get going."

She's right. Our connection and compatibility are rare. Things are good between us—so good that I feel like I need to tell her what happened with Heather.

"I'm not giving up on anything," I say. "I *do* want to minimize the risks to you, but . . . otherwise I'm all in. And again, I'm sorry for being . . . distant."

She takes my hand in hers and squeezes it.

"What if when this case is over, we go away for a couple of days?" I say.

"That would be . . . lovely," she says. "Think your probation officer would let you? I hear she's a real cunt mistress."

"A what?"

"That's what Paul Darren Todd called me."

"You got to talk to him?" I ask.

She nods. "If you hadn't gone AWOL on me the past few days, I would've told you."

Paul Darren Todd is the convicted child molester who was living at Flamingo South when Leah went missing. He's back in prison now where I couldn't get to him. As a probation officer, Lexi has the ability to get inside the state prison system pretty easily and had volunteered to interview him for me.

"And he called you a cunt mistress?"

"Among other things."

"Exactly what is a cunt mistress?" I ask.

"I have no idea, but it's going on my resume."

"What'd he have to say?"

"A lot. Couldn't get him to shut up. He's a sick fucker, but . . . I don't think he had anything to do with what happened to Leah. He's got an alibi for that night that checks out. Most of the twisted shit he's done involves little boys, not girls, and he's never shown any signs of violence, never beat let alone killed any of the kids. Just fucked up their lives forever. Kyle and the other boys were far more at risk from him than Leah."

"Okay, thanks," I say. "We'll—"

"Is that her?" she asks, as Chrissy Violet walks out of Adam's Eve with a backpack slung over her shoulder.

FORTY-EIGHT

"Richard Iversen died a few minutes ago," Pete says.

"Damn," I say. "I was hoping we could interview him before he did."

Lexi and I are in my car in the parking lot of the Gulf Breeze apartment complex off Back Beach Road on the east end of the beach not far from the Hathaway Bridge.

It's a small, old complex in need of a remodel and new paint. It's probably the cheapest place to live on the beach. Chrissy Violet resides alone in 4B, a tiny loft apartment on the ground floor with a view of the mailboxes and dumpsters.

"Guess he's taking his secrets to the grave," Pete says. "If he has any."

That gives me an idea.

"Oh, he has some," I say.

"Yeah, you're probably right."

"Thanks for letting me know," I say. "I appreciate it."

"No problem. I'm still looking into him. Let you know if anything turns up."

"I think it's possible a woman named Chrissy Violet might

have something to do with Blade's disappearance. Could you look into her?"

"Sure. Who is she?"

I tell him.

"I'll see if she's got a record."

"See if she has any properties where she might be holding them. She lives in a small apartment and it's hard to see how she could have them here."

"You're there now?"

"Yeah."

"Want me to join you?"

"Just watching the place right now," I say. "Be more helpful if you look into her."

"I'm on it."

"Sad," Lexi says when I end the call.

"*Iversen?*" I ask in surprise.

"What? No. Chrissy. Sad little life she's living, isn't it? Work a shift at the sex store and come home alone to a shitty little apartment."

"Yeah."

I wonder how little and sad my life might seem to someone looking at it from the outside, how less meaningful and fulfilling it would actually be if I didn't have Blade and Alana, Ashlynn, Pete, and Lexi, if I didn't have work I find challenging and stimulating, if I didn't have music.

"'Most people lead lives of quiet desperation and go to the grave with the song still in them,'" I say.

She nods. "We're capable of so much and . . . do so little. Use so little of our brains, so rarely tap into our subconscious. We blink and it's all over."

Chrissy walks out of her apartment building and toward her car.

I'd like to get a look inside her apartment while she's gone but need to follow her in case she could lead us to Blade and Rush.

"I would say I could take a look at her apartment then Uber to my car or to you afterward," she says, "but I can't commit B and E, even for a good cause."

"I'd never ask you to," I say.

"I appreciate that. I do understand that you don't always operate strictly speaking inside the law, though I often wonder where the line is. I mean, which if any lines you won't cross, but—"

"Not many when it comes to getting Blade back," I say.

She nods. "I figured. But in general . . . I hope you give it some careful consideration and that you do have lines you won't cross. I'd hate to think you believe because of your work you're above or outside the law in some way."

"Conversation for another time," I say. "If she has Blade, I'm going to do whatever I have to to find her and get her back. Do you want to Uber back to your car now in case things get . . ."

"I probably should," she says. "It's bad enough I know you're doing them, but . . . participating is another thing altogether."

"I understand," I say. "Text me when you're safely back at your car. I'll call you later."

She gives me a quick kiss and hops out.

I then follow Chrissy Violet out of the complex and onto Back Beach Road heading west.

FORTY-NINE

I'm in my office the next morning yawning a lot when Lexi calls.

"It's a good thing you left when you did last night," I say.

"Why? What happened?"

"She drove to the dollar store and rented a movie out of the Redbox."

"Oh."

"She then drove home and stayed in the rest of the night."

"I should've stayed," she says. "Sorry."

"No, you—"

Dimitri and Bogdan walk into my office.

I open the top desk drawer on the right where Blade keeps a loaded .38.

"I've got to go," I say. "I'll call you back in a little while."

"Is everything o—"

I end the call, bring up the voice recorder app, press the record button, place the phone on the desk, and rest my hand on the top right drawer.

"Hey, guy," Dimitri says as they sit down. "Zere is no need

for zat." He nods toward the open desk drawer. "Vee are just here for talk."

Just like the last time I saw them, Dimitri is dressed in an expensive black suit with a black silk shirt unbuttoned halfway down his chest and Bogdan is wearing an Adidas black track suit with three white stripes on the sides of the arms and legs.

"So talk," I say.

"Vhere is your partner? Zee Negress with knife."

I wonder if he's asking because he doesn't know or because he does. He seems genuinely curious.

"She's busy slicing up some other Russians today," I say.

"Bogdan, vatch door to make sure she does not sneak een and slit our zroats."

Bogdan turns his chair sideways so he can see me, Dimitri, and the door.

Dimitri shakes his head. "You two . . . are very beeg pain een my zroat."

"You dealt the play," I say. "All I did was get a lap dance."

"Vhat means 'dealt play'?"

Bogdan mimics dealing cards.

"I am here to deal 'nozher play," Dimitri says.

His accent is thick and difficult to understand.

"Dimitri declares truce," he says. "No more bad blood. No more shoot car and no more cut on Dimitri or Bogdan. You tell partner, okay, guy?"

I grab the pen next to the yellow legal pad on the desk and pretend to write as I recap. "No more shoot car. No more stab Russians."

"Zat is rrright," he says. "Vrite down and tell partner."

"Got it," I say.

"Be sure to tell her."

"I will."

"And, guy, know zis," he says. "Zis ees—how do you say?—

official vord. Real talk is zis. My old uncle vill not always be around, vill not always be een charge. One day . . . vhen he ees not looking . . . Dimitri vill punch your ticket."

"I don't doubt you'll try," I say. "And who knows . . . back-shooter like you . . . you may get lucky and take us out, but know this—if you do, my partner and I have people on both sides of the law that will square it. People who will dismantle your life piece by piece. Not hired help like you have—" I nod toward Bogdan "—but people who consider us family and won't stop until you're in so much pain death will be a welcome relief when it comes, and it will come. So if you come after us, just make sure it's worth your life, because that's what it will cost you."

Bogdan shifts in his chair and starts for his gun but stops.

I turn to see Bobby Doll standing in the doorway with a sawed-off shotgun.

Ben must have called him. I had let both Ben and Bobby know what was going on and had Bobby on standby, but with Blade missing, Ben must have called him the moment Dimitri and Bogdan walked into the building.

Dimitri turns to look at him.

Bobby Doll isn't much to look at—a small white twenty-something with pale skin, disconcerting green eyes, and a buzzcut he does himself—but he's good with a gun and enjoys using it like no one I've ever seen. Blade and I had helped him out more than a few times when we were all kids in the system, and though there's nothing he won't do for us, it's making a mess of bad guys that he most enjoys.

He moves into the room and in a disquietingly whispered voice says, "No need to live with a threat hangin' over you, Burke. Let me just finish it now."

"I know what you're sayin'," I say. "And I appreciate it. But you know what a mess your shotgun makes. Remember how long it took to clean up all that blood spatter and brain matter last time. And we still didn't get it all."

"We could take 'em somewhere," he says.

Dimitri says, "May we go now?"

I nod.

Dimitri stands slowly, his arms out as if he's being held up or arrested. Bogdan does the same.

And they walk that way out of the office, neither of them even glancing in Bobby Doll's direction.

FIFTY

That afternoon while Chrissy Violet is at work I break into her apartment.

Though not an expert at B and E, I have no problem gaining access to her place and not leaving any sign that I jimmied the lock.

Inside, I discover that the apartment is even smaller and sadder than I had imagined.

Standing just inside the door, I can see the entire apartment. I scan it as I pull on latex gloves.

A small living room area holds only a couch, coffee table, and TV on a stand against the wall. The left wall has a small, short staircase leading up to an open bedroom loft. An open kitchen and a tiny bathroom, the door open, are beneath the loft.

There's not much in it, but what is present is so neat and orderly as to be the master work of someone with obsessive-compulsive disorder.

The light gray walls are mostly empty. The only things

hanging on them are a few framed prints of sexually explicit lesbian art.

The apartment and its condition say a lot about her personality and need for control.

Searching a more messy and disorderly place would be much easier—at least in terms of leaving evidence that the place has been searched. I'll have to be extremely careful if I'm not going to leave any signs that I was here.

It's obvious that Blade and Rush aren't here. The two things I've got to discover is if they have been at some point and any clues to where they might be now—if she has them or has anything to do with their disappearances.

I quickly check the bathroom to make sure no one is hiding behind the shower curtain, then make my way up the stairs to the loft.

I start with the closet.

Sliding the light, hollow white door open, I first make sure no one is inside. After determining no one is there, I examine the precisely folded clothes, trying not to move them. Even though the closet is minuscule, Chrissy has so few clothes, she has room to spare.

I check all the pockets. They are all empty.

The suitcase against the left wall is empty.

The rack of shoes on the right are clean. There's no sand, dirt, or mud to indicate that she has gone anywhere besides work and home and the dollar store.

The suitcase on the only shelf, which is above the rod the clothes are hanging on, is empty, as is the duffle bag beside it.

Next to the duffle bag is a shoebox with an old .22 stainless steel pistol and a box of ammo in it. I lift the weapon, smell it, examine it closely. It's clean. There are no signs that it has been fired recently.

The full bed takes up most of the space in the loft bedroom. On one side of it there's a nightstand with a lamp, a book of lesbian erotica, a dildo, some lube, a clock radio, and a small air purifier. The other bedside table is actually a faux wooden two-drawer filing cabinet. The only thing on top of it is a charging station. Inside the drawers are all her papers and documents—birth certificate, social security card, title to her car, and her banking information, which includes a checking account, a very modest savings account, and a five-thousand-dollar debt consolidation loan.

There are a few other documents and papers, some correspondence, but nothing related to whether she might have anything to do with Blade's or Rush's disappearance. No deeds to other properties she owns, no leases for rental properties. Nothing. The only other thing in the drawers is some very disturbing and violent lesbian erotic fan fiction that at quick glance includes some truly sick fantasies.

Finding nothing under the bed, I go back downstairs and search the kitchen, bathroom, and living room.

A few minutes later, I exit the tiny apartment with no evidence that Chrissy even knows Rush or Blade, let alone has anything to do with their disappearances.

FIFTY-ONE

The next night I sneak into Greenwood Cemetery with Janet Deller.

"I can't tell you how much I appreciate this," I say.

"I just hope we can find that little girl," she says. "And we don't get caught."

Janet Deller is a thirty-something white woman with wiry mouse-brown hair and glasses. She's the wife of Joseph Deller, a client Blade and I helped out of a jam a few years back.

She's also an expert in GPR.

Ground-penetrating radar is a high-frequency electromagnetic pulse used to probe the earth. The radar pulses reflect off various interfaces within the ground and are then detected by the radar receiver. Reflecting interfaces may be anything from soil horizons to groundwater, to rock, to pipes or electric lines, or human remains—any object or interface possessing a contrast to the soil around it that can be detected by the GPR.

The radar signal is sent into the ground by an antenna close to the ground. The reflected signals are then detected, processed, and displayed on a graphic recorder. As the GPR moves across the surface of the ground, the graphic recorder displays results in a radar image of the earth.

"This is exciting," Janet says. "I'm usually lookin' for utility lines."

We are here tonight to test my theory that Leah Harrison is buried beneath Jane Iversen's grave. If the GPR can detect an anomaly in the ground beneath Jane's grave, then I can turn it over to Pete and he can try to get a court order to exhume Jane's grave to see if that is, in fact, where Leah is buried.

We are dressed in all black and wearing gloves. I'm carrying a shovel, Janet, a handheld GPR. She normally uses a larger GPR—one that resembles a push lawnmower—but instead of searching from above the ground, we will be scanning from within the ground.

Tomorrow is Richard Iversen's funeral and committal. Tonight, his plot, which is beside his wife's, is an open grave. This is our one chance to get as close as possible to the spot where I believe Leah's remains are.

I climb down into the grave and then help her down.

"You think the remains are beneath Jane Iversen's grave, right?" she says. "Buried in her open grave the night before her burial."

"That's my theory."

"Then we need to dig down a few feet to the approximate depth Leah's small body would've been placed."

"My guess is about three feet," I say.

She nods. "Sounds about right. Just dig right next to the side where Jane's grave is—and you don't have to come this way very far. Just give me enough room to run my device across the side of the soil."

I begin digging.

This is the part that I believe puts us at the greatest risk.

It's a felony to dig up or desecrate a grave. I read the statute earlier today.

Every person who shall knowingly and willfully dig up, except as otherwise provided by law, obliterate, or in any way desecrate any cemetery where human dead are interred, or cause through word, deed or action the same to happen, shall upon conviction be imprisoned for not more than one (1) year in the county jail or fined not more than Five Hundred Dollars ($500.00), or both, in the discretion of the court.

We're not digging up or in any way desecrating a grave, but it certainly appears as if we are, and if we're caught we will most likely be arrested and charged for as much.

"Remember," Janet says, "the best we can hope for is a parabola shape or anomaly in the earth. We know for sure what it is if we find anything like that at all. Often what we get are squiggly lines the shapes of A's where the ground water is flowing around the object."

"If the body of a little ten-year-old girl was buried in the ground without a coffin or anything, will there be something for the GPR to pick up over twenty years later?"

"Absolutely," she says. "Even if the remains are completely decomposed, the bones will show up."

"I know this is a long shot," I say as I dig, "but it's the best theory I've got right now, and if her remains are not here I'll know to look somewhere else. I can't tell you how much I appreciate you doing this—especially with the risks involved."

"Happy to help," she says. "That should be deep enough."

I stop digging and move to the other side of the rectangular opening in the ground.

She straps the small GPR to her hand and says, "Moment of truth."

She moves over to the trench I've just dug beside Jane Iversen's grave, gets on her hands and knees, reaches down into the trench, and begins sliding the device against the side of the earth.

"I'm just going to scan it quickly," she says. "Not look at the readings or anything else. So we can put the dirt back in and get the hell out of here."

"Perfect," I say.

It doesn't take her long to make the scan.

As soon as she's finished, I quickly shovel the dirt back into the trench and smooth it over.

I then toss the shovel up onto the ground and climb out.

Reaching down, I help her climb out, and we rush toward the fence we had climbed over to get into the cemetery earlier.

As we do, she says, "I took a quick look at the findings while you were putting the dirt back in. There's definitely an anomaly under Jane's grave. Burke, I think your theory is right. I'll be shocked if that's not Leah's remains under there."

FIFTY-TWO

"You found her," Heather is saying.

"We won't know that for sure for a few days," I say, "but I wanted you to know where we are with everything and what is happening."

We are back on her balcony, the bright white beach below us, the seemingly infinite green Gulf before us.

"What *is* happening?" she asks.

"The Bay County Sheriff's Office has all my work, theories, and the GPR graph showing the anomaly beneath Jane Iversen's grave. Hopefully, they are taking it seriously and will take the next steps with the case."

"Which are?"

"They'll call in FDLE to conduct their own GPR readings and if they agree with our findings, then they'll get a court order to exhume."

"All this time . . ." she says. "Buried that close to where her backpack was found. It makes sense. But . . . Richard? How . . . and why?"

"We . . . won't know until . . . If they find her there, there will be an autopsy. Our hope is that it will give us insight into what happened. And there's always the chance that Iversen left a note or journal entry behind, some form of confession. We just won't know until . . . And there's still a chance that it's not her remains but something else beneath Jane's grave."

"It's her," she says. "I can . . . feel it. It's my baby and you . . . . found her. I can never thank you enough."

"There's still a lot more that has to be done—and much of it is out of my hands—but . . . I think we're . . . We're . . . There's movement in the case . . . and it's heading in what I believe is the right direction."

"But . . ." she says.

"What is it?"

"I don't understand," she says. "How would Richard have . . . When did he . . . Did he know she was out there in that storm? Did he go after her or did he . . . just happen on her somehow? It doesn't make sense."

A gull glides by just a few feet from the balcony railing and lets out a loud, long shriek, and she jumps.

"You okay?" I ask.

"Yeah," she says. "Sorry. Thought I was in an Alfred Hitchcock film for a minute. I remember . . . There was one time when Leah and I were out here and a gull flew by—even closer than that one—and she lunged to try to catch it. She would've gone over the rail if I hadn't grabbed her. She was always . . . so in the moment, did everything with such reckless abandon . . . She was truly a wild child, but she was also so sweet. There were times when she'd snuggle with me and just out of the blue she'd say some of the sweetest things. Just melt your heart—all the more so because she rarely said them and you knew if she did . . . she meant them."

I nod and wait.

Eventually, she wipes her eyes and says, "Does it make any sense to you?"

"The Iversen grave?" I ask. "I have a few ideas, but that's all they are, just some theories."

"Well, your others have been right so far."

"We don't know that for sure yet," I say. "And—"

"God, I wish I could remember that night," she says. "I can't believe I'm so useless."

A sudden flash of an idea streaks across the dark sky of my mind and I wonder if there might be a way to unlock her memories that have remained imprisoned all this time.

"Would you be willing to undergo hypnotherapy to see what you might remember?" I ask.

"I'd be willing to do anything, but . . ."

"It might not work," I say, "but I think it'd be worth a try."

"Oh, it'll work," she says. "I've been under before. But I just don't think there's many memories in there to access. I was asleep when everything happened."

"I'm not sure you were," I say.

"What do you—"

"All I have are theories," I say, "but I think your lack of memory is not from drinking too much, but from being drugged. I think the reason you can't remember anything at all is because Victor Dunkel gave you something, probably GHB or some other type of date rape drug. Probably gave it to several of y'all—maybe everybody. I think that was his MO for the parties, why he hosted and provided the alcohol."

"Oh my God," she says. "Makes sense. He was so creepy. I don't know anyone who would've slept with him by choice."

"The thing is . . . if you were drugged . . . because of the presence of the drug, you probably weren't able to make full memories. At best you'll probably have flashes. But whatever is in your subconscious . . . hypnotherapy should help you access it."

Tears fill her eyes. "Do you have any . . . idea . . . how relieved . . . If I wasn't . . . If it wasn't something I did, but . . . something that was . . . Do you know someone who can put me under and help me remember?"

I nod. "I do. She's very good."

"I'd like to do it as soon as possible."

"I'll set it up."

"Do you have any other theories?" she asks.

I shrug. "Maybe a few more that are trying to form," I lie.

I'm afraid if I tell her any more, she will back out and refuse to undergo hypnosis—not that I know much, but I suspect she's more involved than she thinks she is.

"I'll set everything up and be in touch," I say.

She reaches up and touches my face, her eyes brimming with tears. "You . . . are . . . an . . . angel sent to us. Thank you."

If I'm right, she won't think that after the hypnotherapy session, but I just nod and smile and say, "Thank you."

FIFTY-THREE

Later that night I'm in my car watching Chrissy Violet's apartment when Pete calls.

I'm still following Chrissy when I can because I'm not convinced she's not responsible for Blade's and Rush's disappearances and because I don't know what else to do.

Since it's just me and I'm still working Leah's case, I haven't been on Chrissy twenty-four hours a day, so I can't say for sure she hasn't done anything suspicious or hasn't been where Blade and Rush are. What I *can* say is that she hasn't done any of those things while I have been following her.

This feels like a waste of time, and it probably is, but so much of this work feels that way, and like I say, I don't know what else to do.

"My supervisor found your work and theory convincing," Pete says. "Sheriff signed off on it. FDLE did their own scan. And Judge Thomas signed the order. Exhumation happens tomorrow."

"That's great," I say. "Thanks, man."

"For what?"

"All your help, letting me know. Everything."

"Thank *you* for doing our job for us."

"Even if she is under that grave," I say, "gotta find out how she got there, what happened to her, who's responsible."

"Sure," he says, "but if she's there, the fact that she's there—in that location—will tell us a lot, and an autopsy may tell us the rest."

"Hopefully."

"Well more than we know now."

"Be hard to know less," I say.

"Anything happening with Chrissy Violet?" he asks.

"Not really," I say. "The only thing that might be something . . . and it's a very big *might*, is she's been shopping for new household stuff. New bedspread. New wall art. New bathroom and kitchen things. Almost like she's building a new nest or getting ready for company. Or a new bride. It's a long shot. And it's thin as hell, but . . . it's all I got."

"Could be something," he says. "I've got something too. Well, for you. There's nothing I can do with it. And to be clear, I'm not in any way suggesting you commit any more B and E. This is even thinner than what you got—and that's sayin' something—but . . . it's the only thing I've been able to find."

"What is it?"

"She's got a snowbird uncle who lives in Michigan half the year and here half the year," he says. "He rents when he's here, so he doesn't have a place here but he does keep a storage unit year-round. No way I could get a warrant to take a look into it, but . . . if she has them . . . could be there."

"Where?"

"Safe Self-Storage on Back Beach," he says. "Unit 557."

FIFTY-FOUR

According to its website, Safe Self-Storage is committed to providing affordable prices for all your mini self-storage needs. Conveniently located and locally owned, they offer safe, clean, secure, and easily accessible self-storage units.

What it doesn't mention is a resident on-site manager. What it does mention is a video surveillance system.

I drive pass the location very slowly and take a good look at it.

It's a typical mid-tier self-storage place—rows of long tin buildings with roll-up garage-style doors, surrounded by a cement and iron security fence. American and Florida flags fly out front on tall metal poles, lit from beneath by tepid flood-lights, and tall, open bay units in the back house campers, boats, and RVs.

Getting over the fence will be no problem.

Getting over the fence without being seen or recorded will be.

After casing the joint during several passes back and forth

on Back Beach, I park in a hotel parking lot across the street and watch it for a while.

After over two hours, no one has come or gone.

When I leave the hotel, I drive over to the Walmart on Front Beach. Putting on a cap and a pair of shades, walking stooped over and with a slight limp and my head down, I go in and buy gloves, a small black gym bag, a black balaclava, and a pair of bolt cutters. I pay cash using self-checkout so a clerk doesn't look at the items I'm purchasing and say something like, "Nice cat burglar kit."

I drive back over to Back Beach Road and pull down a wooded side street. Park in the lot of a closed pest control place, grab my cat burglar kit, and run into the woods behind Safe Self-Storage.

When I near the back of the storage place, I put on the gloves and mask and come up behind it. Reaching the fence, I search along it for the security cameras and try to find the spot that seems the least covered.

Tossing the gym bag over, I quickly scale the eight-foot mostly for show fence.

Inside the compound, I scan the site from the back corner of an RV. Seeing no one, I read the numbers on the buildings—each is the range of the storage units it holds.

Running to the third building to the right, I round the back corner and see that 557 is two units from the end.

It's a 10x10 unit with a roll-up door and combination lock at the bottom.

I quickly remove the bolt cutters from the gym bag and cut through the lock.

As soon as I can slide the broken lock out of the hasp, I pull a flashlight out of my bag and push open the door.

Inside, I find Blade and Rush bound and gagged and

surrounded by cardboard boxes, plastic storage bins, and random small furnishings and appliances.

As if part of some kinky sex party or the centerpiece of an erotic art installation, they are restrained with elaborate BDSM items from Adam's Eve—bondage ropes, leather cuffs and shackles, fetish collars, and the like. They are tied to large X-shaped bondage devices, their hands and feet spread and bound to each of the four corners, and each of them has a pink leather pig mask over their head, and a black leather ball gag in their mouth.

A sense of relief rushes over me when I see that they are both breathing, though with how they are bound and gagged it's hard to see how.

I rush over and begin to untie Blade.

"It's me," I say.

I untie the ball gag and it falls to the floor. I then unsnap and remove her mask.

"The fuck took you so damn long?" she asks, her voice soft and hoarse, her mouth dry.

"Haven't had my partner. She's been tied up."

"I hear her ass is the brains and the brawn of the operation."

"Oh, shit," I say.

"What?"

"I need to get a picture of you like this before I untie you."

"Bitch, I will dick-stab you if you do," she says. "Quit fuckin' around and get me the hell out of this shit."

I'm working on freeing her wrists when I sense someone behind us and then—a jolt.

Every muscle in my body tenses and seizes and cramps and spasms. Pain shoots through me like a billion needles being simultaneously jabbed into every inch of me.

As I fall to the cement floor, I'm confused and can't understand what's going on.

FIFTY-FIVE

When the fog begins to clear, I can see that Chrissy is trying to restrain Blade's left arm.

"Be still or I'll tase you," Chrissy says.

Her voice is soft and a little squeaky and shows no emotion.

Blade keeps reaching to the back of the leather pig mask that Chrissy must have somehow forced back on.

"Stop it," Chrissy says.

I can tell Chrissy thinks Blade is trying to take the mask off, but I know better.

Since early adolescence, Blade has kept several knives and blades on her person—in her clothes, shoes, hair, and on her body. It's where her nickname comes from. She began it because of the prevalence of sexual assault in the foster care and children's homes we were in, but she has continued it to this day because of the prevalence of assault and battery, sexual and otherwise, everywhere.

"Last chance," Chrissy says. "Be still or I'll—"

Blade finally gets her hand beneath the mask and comes

out with one of the little utility knife blades she hides in her hair.

She slices Chrissy's wrist.

Chrissy squeals and drops the stun gun.

She clutches at the cut with her other hand and Blade swipes at her some more, blindingly finding her other arm and the side of her face.

Chrissy screams and begins to cry.

I still don't have full use of my muscles, but I rock back and forth until I can roll. I roll over toward Chrissy and knock her feet out from underneath her.

When she hits the ground, I roll on top of her and press her down with all my weight.

She continues to cry and scream as she begins to hit me and tries to push me off her, but she is unable to budge me, and she can't keep hitting because she has to hold her wrist to try to stop the bleeding.

While this is happening, Blade cuts her right arm free, then removes her mask.

Once she removes the mask and ball gag, she bends down and frees her feet.

When she is off the X, she walks over and picks up the stun gun. She then rolls me off Chrissy and stuns the shit out of her.

"That's enough," I say. "You're going to kill her."

"Yes, I am," she says. "But not like this."

Eventually, she stops, leaving the seemingly unconscious Chrissy and making her way over to free Rush.

"Call Pete," I say. "She'll go away for a very long time."

She shakes her head.

"Blade," I say.

"No," she says.

"You don't want this on your conscience or hanging over you."

"She won't be on my conscience," she says. "And I promise you this—no one will ever find her."

"They don't have to find her to prosecute you," I say. "Please. Listen to me. Fuck her up. Hurt her. Bad. But don't kill her. Let Pete arrest her. Please."

"She'll just do it again," she says. "But that's not even why. I can't let her do what she did to me and keep breathing. I can't."

I can't say what I really want to, not in front of Rush. If Blade does what she's contemplating doing, Rush will know. Rush will be a witness. I don't think Rush would ever turn on and testify against Blade, but I can't know that for sure. Rush could fold under pressure if she's questioned about it, or she could get popped for drugs or a domestic or a DUI or anything and use her knowledge of what Blade does to Chrissy as her Get Out of Jail Free card.

"I understand," I say. "I do. And I don't care about her. Anything you do to her is too good for her, but I know what it's like to have something always hanging over you. I know what it's like to be inside. I don't want any of that for you."

"I know," she says, "and I appreciate it. But I can't let this go. I can't."

When she takes off Rush's mask, Rush is crying.

"You okay?" Blade asks.

Rush shakes her head.

"You will be," she says. "Take a minute. But you will be."

Rush looks down at Chrissy.

"Look at me," Blade says. "I'm gonna kill her."

"Good."

"That okay with you?"

She nods.

"Will you ever tell?"

"Never," she says. "I swear. No matter what. I'll help you so I'll be guilty too. So you can trust me."

I wonder if Rush's readiness to help Blade put Chrissy in the ground has more to do with her history of stalking her or what she has done to them while they've been her prisoners. It's an extreme reaction which I have to believe is predicated on Chrissy's extreme behavior and Rush's belief that it will never stop. But no matter how relentless Chrissy has been or what she has done to them in captivity they're making a huge mistake to kill her and they will come to regret it.

And just because Rush is going to help Blade doesn't mean that she couldn't still testify against her, but it does make it less likely and more problematic for prosecutors if it ever comes to that.

"That's my girl," Blade says. "Okay, let's get Burke out of here and break in the office and take the surveillance system before we do anything else."

FIFTY-SIX

"How're you feeling?" I ask Blade as I hand her a cup of coffee.

"Like I don't want to talk," she says.

We each remove the plastic lids from the paper cups and blow onto the coffee, steam rising up to warm our faces.

We're sitting on the top of an old wooden picnic table, our feet on the bench, beneath a pavilion in St. Andrews Marina.

The early morning air is chilly, the sun obscured by a bank of clouds, and a dense, damp fog permeates the atmosphere.

In the distance, two men and a woman fish from the guardrail, as just beneath the fog the waters of the bay undulate and wave.

The hazy breeze blowing in off the bay carries on its currents the disembodied shrieks of gulls and the clanging sounds of sailboat riggings. From somewhere in the unseen distance a low, long foghorn blows, sounding forlorn as a train whistle.

We sip our coffee and take it all in.

Neither of us have slept, and behind our bloodshot eyes we are weary and irritable.

"You ain't gonna get me to say you were right," she says.

"Not tryin' to."

"Not about to regret takin' that bitch off the board. Not now. Not ever. Man, fuck her."

Tears well up in her tired eyes but don't crest her lids and come out.

"Wasn't just the imprisonment," she says. "How helpless, powerless, and little she made me feel. It was the . . . humiliation. The things she did to me. She was so . . . small . . . so mousy with her squeaky fuckin' voice and . . ."

She trails off, blinks several times, and drinks some more of her coffee.

"I'm so sorry," I say. "And I'm sorry I didn't get there sooner."

"Yeah," she says, her tone changing, lightening. "The fuck you been doin'?"

"Spinnin' my wheels," I say. "Been lost without you."

"You still been workin' the Harrison case?"

I nod.

"Gettin' anywhere?"

I shrug. "Maybe."

"Let's hear it."

"Before we get to that," I say. "You ever need to talk about . . . any of it . . . don't think I'll be righteous because I asked you not to. I won't. I swear. I would've done the same thing."

"No you wouldn't have," she says. "Your ass might have killed her in a blind fuckin' fury in the heat of the moment, but not later, not in cold blood—only in hot."

She's right. I'm rage and she's revenge.

"Tell me what's happenin' in this case you ain't gettin' paid for," she says.

I tell her about my theory, about Iversen dying, about Janet helping me with the GPR, and the exhumation.

"Fuck you," she says with genuine warmth and appreciation. "You gonna solve that shit without me. Man . . . fuck you."

"Not solved yet," I say. "Won't know until later this morning if she's even in there. And even if she is . . . unless she has a crushed skull or something, we still won't know how she died or what happened."

"Be a hell of a lot closer to knowin'."

I tell her about my theory that Victor Dunkel served date rape drugs at his party and that might have impacted Heather's memory, and her willingness to undergo hypnosis.

"Shit, bitch, you been busy," she says, more of her personality and swagger coming back. "My ass needs to get abducted more often. You been too busy to finger any strippers, or did you fit that shit in too?"

I laugh, then tell her about my meeting with Lev and then later with Dimitri and Bogdan.

"No wonder you didn't have time to find my ass sooner," she says. "You been a busy boy."

And because I believe it will cheer her up even further and decrease any additional distance between us, I say, "I haven't fingered any strippers, but I did fuck Heather Harrison—well, she fucked me."

"Wait. *Whaaaa?* Back that shit up again and run it by me one more time. Slow. With details. Work it. Flip it. And reverse it. Go."

My confession achieves the desired effect.

"She definitely the one that did the fuckin'," she says. "Your ass got raped more than mine did. Shee-it. And I suppose even though you were an innocent bystander in that little . . . encounter, you've already confessed to Lexi a few hundred times."

I shake my head. "Not yet."

"There may be hope for you after all," she says.

"If we stay together and get serious I will, but—"

"Spoke too soon," she says. "You ain't learned shit. Good thing I'm back to continue your education."

"Yes it is," I say. "And not a moment too soon."

FIFTY-SEVEN

"You were right," Pete says. "She was buried beneath Jane Iversen's grave."

I let out a sigh of relief. I hadn't realized it but I had been holding my breath while we spoke.

Blade gives me a look of appreciation and a nod.

We are in a booth in the back of Thai Basil on Beck in St. Andrews having lunch. It's midafternoon and we have the place to ourselves. I'm having chicken red curry, Pete's having sushi, and Blade is eating panang curry.

"Obviously, we don't have a positive ID yet, but it's the remains of a pre-teen female, so . . ."

"How long will an ID take?" Blade asks.

"Shouldn't take too long. They'll probably do dental and DNA. The remains were in a bag so they're well preserved."

She nods.

"How are you doing?" he asks.

"I'm a'ight," she says.

"Y'all haven't said anything about last night or—"

"Best you don't know any of it," I say.

"Shit," he says. "Well, I'm glad you're okay. Good to have you back."

I wait a beat then return to talking about the case—and not only to change the subject but because I want to know.

"Could they tell what she was wearing?" I ask.

"Said a dark cropped hoodie sweatshirt and sweatpants kind of thing," he says. "They used words like *hip hop, jogging suit* and *dance wear*—whatever any of that means."

Blade says, "Means my girl had style."

"May mean something else too," I say. "When are they doing the autopsy?"

"Got some kind of specialist coming into town tomorrow," he says. "Forensic anthropologist or something like it, but . . . I asked one of the FDLE techs that was there today if there were any obvious signs of anything and she said it looks like her skull was fractured. Say it's probably all they're going to find and was most likely the cause of death."

I think about how that fits with everything else.

The lady in charge approaches our table. I'm not sure if she's the owner or manager or what, but I do know she's in charge. She's a middle-aged Asian lady with shortish black hair and glasses she has to keep pushing up her nose.

"How is everything, honey?"

"Fantastic as usual," I say.

"Very good," Pete says.

Blade nods.

"What's wrong with you?" she asks Blade. "Long night, honey?"

"Yes, ma'am," Blade says. "Need a nap. Or a vacation."

"You and me both, honey," she says, and walks off.

"I'm going to notify the family of what we have so far," Pete says when she is gone.

"Can you delay doing that?" I ask.

"By how long?" he asks. "Maybe by minutes or hours, but not by days."

"Just a few hours," I say. "Heather is undergoing hypnotherapy this evening and I think the closer she hears what you have to say to when she goes under the better. And I have an idea."

"Oh hell," Blade says. "He has an idea."

"Care to share it with us?" Pete asks. "Or is it something I don't want to know?"

"Nothing illegal," I say. "Just ill-advised. Since we now have a body, it's going to really shake things up. It's the perfect time to confront the killer. We were going to try to unlock Heather's memories anyway. Let's try to get everybody together and do a walk-through of that night. Tell them it's to help Heather remember what she can."

"Iversen didn't do it?" Pete says.

"I don't think so, but . . .

"You know who did it, don't you?" Blade says.

"Just have ideas," I say. "And I think this is the best way to test them."

"But you know who did it, don't you?"

FIFTY-EIGHT

"I don't believe Leah ever left this condo alive on the night she disappeared," I say.

I'm speaking to the assembled group in the spot where they had the hurricane party near the pool at Flamingo South. Though we are several feet from the pool, which is surrounded by a wrought iron fence, the smell of chlorine permeates the air.

Pete notified Heather, Malcolm, and Kyle about the body a few minutes before. Heather is still crying.

The family is surrounded by those willing to join us for this little experiment in memory—including Victor Dunkel, Marjorie and Arthur Whitten-Collins, Brian Meeks, Heather's Uncle Frank, Miss Barbara, Reg and Val Scott, Erik and Sadie Arnold. Blade, Pete, and Shereen stand to the side.

Shereen King is a family therapist who specializes in hypnotherapy.

Everyone is dressed casually and, as if they've come straight from work, Reg and Val have flour and tomato sauce on their clothes.

The cement condo rises above us, its topmost floors disappearing into the night sky.

"I thought she broke into my storage unit," Marjorie Whitten-Collins says.

"I don't think she did," I say. "Some of the things found there were hers, but I don't think she took them there that night. She spent plenty of time there—as did her friends. Everything found there can be explained being there without her going there that night."

Behind the group, next to the closed condo rental office, the Coke machine compressor kicks on.

"But the trucker and the storm chaser saw her on Thomas Drive," Reg says.

"They saw someone," I say. "I don't think it was Leah. I don't even think they saw the same person. Dixie Lee Jennings saw someone in a blue shirt or outfit or maybe even pajamas who moved oddly. Ethan Storm saw someone in a yellow rain slicker who he thought was older than Leah. It wasn't until after he heard about Leah going missing that he said it could be her."

"Why would the two witnesses lie?" Malcolm says.

He looks upset like Heather and Kyle, but he also seems nervous, twitchy.

In the moment before I respond, the tide of the unseen Gulf can be heard crashing onto the beach and rolling back out.

"I don't think they did," I say. "If you reread their witness statements, I think you'll see that they saw someone that night —just not Leah. Who is roughly the size of Leah and could look like Leah—especially on a dark and stormy night? I think Ethan saw Heather."

"*Me?*" she says in surprise. "Are you . . . You're serious?"

"Bullshit," Malcolm yells. "We're not gonna stand here and be—

"Hush, Malcolm," Heather says. "I want to hear what he has to say."

"But he's trying to frame you for—"

"I'm not framing anyone," I say. "I'm not even accusing anyone."

Heather and I lock eyes and she nods.

"I want to know the truth," she says. "No matter what it is."

"That's all I want," I say. "If I'm right and Leah never left this place alive, then what happened here that night is even more important. Dr. Shereen King is here to help Heather unlock her memories, but we need your help too. We believe that Heather was drugged that night, which is why she hasn't been able to remember anything, but we're hoping we can change that tonight."

"We were all on drugs that night and every night back then," Victor Dunkel says.

"I didn't say on drugs or doing drugs," I say. "I said *drugged* —without her permission or knowledge."

"That's bullshit," Dunkel says. "And even if she was . . . you couldn't prove it or who did it all these years later."

"You drugged us, didn't you, you creepy little fucker," Malcolm says to Dunkel.

"I didn't. I swear. I'm not gonna stand here and—"

"If you leave you just look even more guilty," Reg says.

"Stay and hear him out," Pete says.

"We're not here to try to prove that she was drugged," I say. "We're here to try to find out exactly what happened that night. And we need your help to do that. We need you to all go to where you were that night around midnight. We've cleared everything with the current tenants. If you were in one of the units, there will be a chair for you right outside the door you can sit on. Just go to where you were beginning around midnight and wait for us there. Investigator Pete Anderson of the Bay County Sheriff's Office has agreed to stand in for Richard Iversen."

"Who's the real killer, right?" Dunkel says.

FIFTY-NINE

"I didn't kill my daughter," Heather whispers to me as we walk toward her condo.

She has slowed her pace to match mine and create a little distance between us and her husband and son.

"I don't think you did," I say.

"I don't know what I did that night," she says, "but I know it wasn't that."

I nod.

"If it was that," she adds, "I'd want to know, but it wasn't that."

She catches up with her family, and we continue—the Harrisons in the front, Shereen and me in the back.

We enter the condo and wait for Shereen to tell us what to do.

"Heather, let's you and I sit over here," she says, pointing to the seating area in the living room. "Why don't y'all sit at the dining table. The main thing is to keep quiet and still."

I sit at one end of the table, Malcolm and Kyle at the other, their hostility toward me palpable.

Only the five of us are in the condo. We didn't want Heather to feel overwhelmed and we didn't want anyone official here, such as Pete.

"Okay, Heather," Shereen says, "get as comfortable as you can. And just relax. You're in a safe place. There's nothing but support and understanding here. The only thing we're here to do is help you remember. Nothing else. Whatever memories you have, whichever ones the drug, if you were drugged, let you make, are in your subconscious, and all we're going to do is access them. Okay?"

Heather nods. "Okay."

"There won't be any gotcha moments," Shereen says. "And I'm not gonna say or do anything other than ask questions—and not leading questions. I won't make any suggestions. We want your pure memories, uninfluenced memories, okay?"

Shereen's voice is soft and has a rhythm and tone and cadence that give it a hypnotic quality.

"I wonder if you'd like to begin," she says.

Heather, who already seems like she's in a trance, nods.

"I wonder if you'd like to stare at a certain spot for me," Shereen says. "How about this light?"

She points to one of the small, recessed pin spotlights in the ceiling.

Heather leans her head back and stares at it.

"Is it too bright?" Shereen asks.

Heather shakes her head.

"Do you notice how your eyes and mind are starting to get tired? Please try not to close your eyes, even though they are so tired. Just keep them fixed on that little light. That's good. You're doing so good. I know you're tired. I know you want to close your eyes, but try to keep them open just a little longer, okay? Once your eyes become misty and your vision blurry you may want to rest your eyes, and if you do that's just fine."

Shereen pauses a moment and Heather closes her eyes.

"Isn't this easy and relaxing?" Shereen asks. "You're doing so well. Just keep relaxing. Let yourself relax more than you ever have. Let relaxation wash over you like a warm wave in the Gulf. Can you feel how good and heavy that wave of relaxation feels as it crashes over you? Do you feel heavier with that wave on top of you?"

Heather nods.

"Now I'd like to invite you to focus on your breathing. Concentrate on each and every breath. I wonder if you would imagine a heavy weighted blanket resting on you, and it feels so good and comfortable and relaxing. And with every breath you take you feel . . . heavier and more . . . relaxed. Slowly and consistently . . . take deep breaths and let them out slowly. And with every one feel yourself getting heavier and heavier, more and more relaxed."

I can feel myself relaxing so much I'm beginning to go into a trance, and I look away and blink several times.

Shereen repeats the process of the breathing and feeling heavier and heavier a few more times.

Eventually, she says, "I wonder if I might help you re-lax even more by counting down from ten to one? And I wonder if with each number you could imagine yourself being covered with heavier and heavier blankets and becoming more and more relaxed."

She slowly counts her down from ten to one, lingering on each number and making sure Heather is going deeper and deeper under.

"So heavy now as you relax and drift . . ." Shereen is saying. "Going further down, drifting, sinking, floating. Remember your subconscious mind can hear everything it needs to. You just relax and let it. You just let these waves wash over you—waves of comfort and relaxation and warmth and heaviness."

When Shereen is convinced Heather is completely under, she says, "I wonder if you'd like to think back to the night of Leah's disappearance?"

"I would," Heather says, nodding slowly.

"What do you remember?"

"Storm coming. Don't want to go to the hurricane party. Worried. Want to stay home and write. Kids being wild and loud. Going to be cooped up with them for a while. Need a break. Malcolm really wants me to go to the party."

"I wonder if you'd like to see the memories of your subconscious as a dream and describe them. Dreams don't have to make sense or be in chronological order. It doesn't matter what it is—just describe it."

"Lame party by the pool. Weather getting bad. Creepy Dunkel lurking. Val flirting with Malcolm. Don't even care. Reg making eyes at me. Me looking away. Everyone feeling bad about Jane Iversen. Feeling sorry for Richard. But not bad or sorry enough not to party. Val thinks we should all go to the funeral. Storm will postpone it. Why do I feel frustrated? Confused? Upset? Can't remember. Why can't I remember anything? What's wrong with me?"

"I know it's frustrating, but it's not your fault. Don't blame yourself. Don't get upset. Just stay relaxed and remember. Just describe what you see. Just say what you think and feel."

"Head hurts. Feel bad. Want to go to bed. Malcolm staying. He's going to fuck Val. Good. I don't care. Just want to be left alone."

Malcolm flinches at that and glances over at Kyle, whose face remains impassive.

"What're you doing here?" Heather asks.

"Who's there?" Shereen asks. "Where are you now?"

"On our floor. Walking to our condo. The wind is picking up. It's starting to rain. Someone is following me."

"Who is it?"

"Get the fuck away from me," she says. "It's creepy Victor Dunkel. No. Stop. He . . . He's touching me. Grabbing. Leave me the fuck alone. He's pushing me up against the door. Trying . . . He's pulling at my clothes. The door is opening. *Mama? What's . . . Are you okay?* Leah opening the door. I shove Victor off. I go inside and shut the door. Bed. So tired."

So now we know that Leah was okay when Heather got back to the condo, but she was awake and up. And Dunkel was around.

Heather didn't mention anything about locking the door. Did she do it and forget or not do it? One of her only memories from that night up until now is locking the door, and I wonder if it was because of the threat Dunkel posed. I hope Shereen will ask, but she doesn't.

"Malcolm wakes me up. Says Leah's missing," Heather says. "Storm is bad. We've got to find her. Come on. So tired. So out of it. Where's my baby?"

I look over at Malcolm. He lied to us. They didn't wake the next morning to find her gone. They knew in the middle of the night. His gaze is fixed on Heather. He doesn't look in my direction.

"I look around our condo, our floor, the building. Can't find her. Weather is very bad. Malcolm hands me a yellow raincoat. Tells me to search the parking lot and the area around it. Rain coming down so hard. The wind is . . . It's difficult to walk. But I've got to find her. Where is she? Why did she go out in this storm? Doesn't make sense. She wouldn't. I can't find her. She's not out here. I'm going back to the condo. Malcolm helps me out of my wet clothes and puts me to bed. Says he'll take care of everything." She goes quiet for a moment. "It's morning. The bed is wet with rainwater. Malcolm's soaking and muddy clothes are piled on the floor next to it."

I remember Malcolm saying they had been so wasted they had peed the bed, but that was a lie to cover the real reason the bed was wet.

I'm still staring at Malcolm, but now I'm not the only one. Shereen and Kyle are too.

SIXTY

"What did you *do*?" Heather is saying.

Shereen has brought her out of her trance and she is now standing over Malcolm.

All eyes in the room are on him.

Kyle has slid his chair away from his dad and is staring at him, searching his face for answers.

Heather is crying, but her anger has overtaken her sadness. Her voice, which still conveys her brokenness, has reached a new depth of devastation and despair.

"Dad, answer her," he says. "What did you do?"

Malcolm is crying now. "There was . . . nothing I could do. She was . . . already gone. I . . . couldn't . . . I was so fucked up. I wasn't thinking straight, but I thought I was. I panicked. I . . . I don't even recognize who I was that night. I don't. I was trying to save our family—what was left of it. I . . . There was nothing I could do for her, but . . . I couldn't let what happened destroy your life too. We couldn't lose you both. I couldn't let . . . I had to at least save one of you."

"Save me from what?" Kyle says. "From who?"

"They would've locked you up for a very long time."

"For what?" Kyle asks. "I didn't do anything."

"Y'all always played so rough. I know you didn't mean to . . . hurt her."

"I didn't hurt her," Kyle says. "I didn't do anything."

"I had to save you. I knew Heather wouldn't understand. How could she?"

"Tell us what happened," I say.

He doesn't look up, doesn't acknowledge me in any way.

"I came in from . . . Val and I had been on the beach. When I looked in the kids' room . . . Leah was gone. I searched around for her. She wasn't there. I was so mad. I was so tired and I wanted to sleep and she did something like this. She was always doing stuff like that. Always on an adventure, always . . . I woke up Heather to help me look for her. But she was so out of it. We looked . . . Couldn't find her. Not sure how long we were gone. When I came back, I looked in to make sure Kyle was okay and that's when I saw her. She was on the floor on the other side of the bed. Her head was . . . bashed in . . . and . . . Kyle's bat was beside her with blood on it."

"*What?*" Kyle says. "No. No way."

"She hadn't been there before," Malcolm says. "I had looked. She must have gone somewhere and while we were looking for her she came back and startled Kyle or something. I know he wouldn't do something like that if . . . I knew he didn't mean to kill her."

"Oh my God," Heather says, sobs shuddering through her.

"I wouldn't," Kyle says. "I didn't. I swear. I didn't do anything to her. I didn't do anything at all."

"I couldn't let him go to prison or juvie or whatever—not even for . . . Not for any amount of time. I knew it would destroy him, destroy us. I knew you'd never forgive him or me. I was trying to save what was left of our family. I know I should've . . . I'm tellin' you, you weren't the only one who had been drugged. I was drunk and high and . . . I remembered about Jane Iversen's open grave. I had taken Richard there earlier that day to deliver some of the flowers and meet with the funeral director—he was so upset and so alone and I felt like it was the neighborly thing to do. I thought . . . I could give Leah a nice burial in sacred ground and Jane could keep her company. I buried her backpack with some of her things nearby so we could . . . I don't know. I wasn't thinking straight. I thought we might get them one day. I don't know. I just . . ."

"You . . . monster," Heather says, and lunges at Malcolm.

She unleashes a barrage of blows with her small fists. He doesn't move. Doesn't look up. Just takes it.

Shereen grabs Heather from behind and pulls her back. I rush over and grab her.

She shrugs us off and falls to the floor sobbing.

Kyle looks up at me. "I swear I didn't do it. I didn't even get up. I didn't go anywhere. My bat was in the living room. We had been playing sock ball. We left everything in there. It wasn't in our room. I never saw it again. Always wondered what happened to it. I figured Leah took it when she went out. I was always glad she did and hoped she used it to protect herself. I never touched it after we played earlier that night. I didn't go out there and get it. I didn't hit her with it. I didn't . . . I never got out of bed. Hook me up to a polygraph. I swear I'm tellin' the truth."

I nod. "I know," I say. "I know you are. I know you didn't kill her."

Malcolm looks up for the first time, his face red and puffy. "He *didn't*?"

"I keep tellin' you that, Dad. I could never do anything like that. How could you even think I could?"

"I thought it was an accident or a . . . that she startled you out of a nightmare or something. I never believed you could do it on purpose."

Heather looks up at me, wiping her eyes. "If he didn't do it, who did?"

SIXTY-ONE

Malcolm jumps up. "I know who."

He runs out of the condo.

We follow.

"Dad, wait," Kyle is saying. "Stop."

He runs down the breezeway to the stairwell.

We continue to follow him—joined now by the others who had been sitting in front of their old condo doors.

"What's going on?" Pete asks.

When Malcolm reaches the bottom of the stairs, he bursts through the big metal door and heads straight for Victor Dunkel, who is standing near the pool.

"You tried to rape my wife and then you killed our little girl," Malcolm yells. "You ruined our lives you sick fuckin'—"

"I didn't. I swear." Dunkel holds his hands up defensively.

Malcolm tackles him and starts hitting him.

Dunkel is crying and flailing and screaming. "I didn't do it. I swear it. You have to believe me. I would never harm a child. Never."

Everyone is gathered around and looking on now.

"Stop him, Mama," Arthur says.

Eventually, Pete and I pull Malcolm off of Dunkel.

We had been in no hurry to do it, and Dunkel's face shows the early signs of the pummeling he just received, red and puffy, abrasions, swelling, and the beginnings of bruises.

He sits there in a blubbering heap.

"I didn't do it," he says. "I . . . did slip some party drugs into . . . some of the drinks . . . but . . . and I did go up and try to . . . get with Heather, but that's it. After they closed that door, I came back down to the party. Everyone saw me. And I never saw Leah again. I swear it."

"He was at the party the whole time after that," Reg says. "I drank with him while Val was with Malcolm. And Malcolm went up before Victor, so . . ."

Dunkel looks up at Heather. "I swear to God I didn't have anything to do with it."

Heather looks at me. I nod.

"I think after Leah let her mother in the condo, she was awake and bored," I say. "Her mom goes to bed and I think she did what she often did—went out looking for something to do. She snuck into another unit and it cost her her life."

"Whose?" Heather asks.

"Leah would never give Arthur her Giga Pet," I say. "Not willingly. It's what everyone said."

"It's true," Sadie says. "She wouldn't."

"But she would give it to you," I say.

She starts to say something but stops, then looks at her dad.

"I think she slipped into your condo that night," I say to Erik, "like she had so many times before—but this time . . . something happened. Maybe it was an accident. Maybe it was . . . something else. But whatever happened . . . you took her back to her condo while Malcolm and Heather were out searching for her—no one locked their doors back then, and even if they did, you all had a key to each other's places. You laid her on the floor beside her bed and put Kyle's bat beside her—after smearing some of her blood on it."

"*Dad?*" Sadie says, looking at Erik in shock and disgust.

"You then took the Giga Pet and some of the other things Leah had left in your place and put them in Marjorie's storage unit to make it look like Arthur was involved."

"Just . . . a couple of things. The rest was already there."

"You," Heather says to Erik.

"*Daddy?*" Sadie says her voice is low and soft and childlike.

"It was an accident," Erik says. "I swear. I didn't mean for any of it to happen. It was an accident, I swear."

He looks at Sadie. "I'm so sorry, baby, but . . . I had to . . . protect you. I had already put you through enough. I . . . I did it for you."

"*Me?*" she says. "You killed my friend for me?"

"No. You know what I meant. I . . . I couldn't have this—" He turns back toward Heather and Malcolm. "She shouldn't've been there in the first place. Why did y'all let her be so . . . If y'all had been better parents, not let her run around like a little heathen all the time. If y'all had fucked around less and spent more time raising your children. I . . . I had way too much to drink at the party. I think I was drugged too. It's all so cloudy. She was just there and startled me. I . . . I just swung and sort of . . . She hit her head. It was an accident. I swear it. There was nothing I could do for her. I couldn't bring her back. But I could keep my Sadie from losing her father. I couldn't abandon her to my crazy ex-wife. I couldn't let some silly accident ruin my Sadie's life, end my practice, let my ex get everything. I couldn't have her being raised by her bitter old bitty of a mother. I couldn't."

I can't tell how much of what he's saying is true, but if it was truly an accident I'd expect him to be more distraught and less defiant.

"You tried to frame me and Arthur," Kyle says.

Malcolm and Heather both lunge at Erik, and we let them.

And when, a little while later, when Pete and I make a move to pull them off him, Blade steps between us and shakes her head.

Eventually, Heather and Malcolm, punched out and exhausted, roll off Erik and sit on the concrete breathing heavily and crying.

Soon the crying turns to sobbing, a sorrow so deep and visceral it's disquieting.

Kyle joins them on the ground, sitting between them and putting an arm around each of them.

Miss Barbara steps over and places her arm around Sadie, who is weeping quietly.

Pete pulls Erik to his feet, cuffs him, and takes him away.

Victor Dunkel recedes into the dark night and disappears, as everyone else presses in around the Harrisons, sitting around them in a circle of solidarity.

SIXTY-TWO

"Do you think it really was an accident?" Heather Harrison asks.

It's three days later and I'm on her balcony with her again.

I wasn't sure I'd find her here, but I was glad when I did.

The sun is bright, the sky is clear, but the day is cool, and the wind blowing in off the Gulf has some bite to it.

I shrug. "I don't think he meant to kill her, but . . . that's not the same as an actual accident."

She nods and seems to think about it as she looks out at the whitecaps tipping the rolling green Gulf waters.

Erik Arnold is still in custody. Pete says he's cooperating. He's already given a full confession and plans to plead guilty in a manslaughter deal to prevent having a trial.

"I'm still having difficulty wrapping my head around all of it," she says.

"It's too much to take in," I say.

"So Richard Iversen . . ." she says.

"Was telling the truth and just wanted to do some good with his money before he died."

"Except he didn't have any," she says.

"Except for that."

"He didn't have anything to do with it or . . ."

"I don't think so," I say. "And I don't think he knew she was buried beneath his wife's grave."

She shakes her head. "I still can't believe Malcolm did . . . what he did. I find that the most shocking of all. I can't . . . forgive him for it. I just can't. We haven't been in a marriage for a long time, not really, but we're finally getting a divorce."

I nod but don't say anything.

"Do you really think Sadie didn't know anything?" she asks.

"No way to know for sure, but I don't think she did."

"Good. She's been so sweet. We've . . . It's been nice to have her around. Hard to believe she's around the age my Leah would be now."

She breaks down and begins to cry.

I step inside to get her some tissues and return to the balcony.

"When I think about . . . all she's missed . . . all she'll never experience . . . It's too much."

I nod slowly and take in the palpable pain emanating from her.

"It's so fuckin' unfair," she says between sniffles.

"It is."

She looks up at me as if something has just occurred to her. "What about the picture?" she asks. "Who is the little girl in the school picture from Leah's backpack?"

I shrug. "We may never know," I say. "But my guess is . . . it was left at the condo by tourists. Leah probably found it and . . . decided to hold onto it in case the little girl ever came back."

"She probably made up an elaborate story about her and used it in some of her make-believe adventures. God, that girl had an imagination on her. It's so . . . cruel that she never got to . . ."

We are quiet for a long moment, the only sounds the Gulf winds and the shrieks of gulls in it.

"Thank you," she says. "You . . . found her for me. You gave her back to me. You . . . took away the relentless torture of not knowing."

Now if I could just do that for myself in Kaylee's case.

"You're my angel," she says. "I'll never forget what you've done for me. You gave me . . . what I most wanted in all the world—except for it never happening in the first place. I want you to know that . . . you . . . I can't explain it exactly because I'm still broken and always will be, but you . . . took away some of my . . . suffering. And I . . . And that's not something I ever thought anyone could do."

SIXTY-THREE

Rush and I are playing an acoustic duo set at the Lie'Brary on Beck. She's still a little shaky and upset by all that happened with Chrissy Violet, but playing her pink guitar in such a cool place with such a chill vibe seems to be helping.

Blade and Lexi are sitting in the audience, but not together. Lexi is here with us but can't be seen to be.

We're in the back area of the literary-themed bar, surrounded by books and people sitting on couches and around tables, many of them with large slices of pizza from the Slice House next door.

We wrap up our second of three sets with a duet of Dylan's "You're Gonna Make Me Lonesome When You Go."

When we arrive at the table, slices of pizza and cold pineapple cider are waiting for us.

Lexi sits at the table next to ours, her chair just behind mine so she can be with us without appearing to be.

"Y'all sound so good together," she says.

"Thanks," I say.

"You're so sweet," Rush says.

I'm having a slice of Thai-Pocalypse and it is a perfect masterpiece of pizza. The cider is ice-cold with just the right amount of sweetness, and my companions are a delight. It's about as good as moments get in my life, and I am grateful for it.

I raise my glass. "To good friends, good food, and good music," I say. "And to Leah Harrison."

We each clink our glasses.

"To us and to Leah," Lexi says.

Blade raises her glass and says, "To our asses finding some paying jobs."

As we near the end of our break, Pete walks in.

"PISTOL PETE," Blade says like a sports announcer.

"Pull up a chair," I say. "What would you like to drink?"

"Can't stay," he says as he sits down. "Just have some info to share."

"Good info or bad info?" Blade asks.

Lexi turns her chair so she's facing us.

"Both, actually," he says. "I have two bad and one good. Which would you like first?"

"You choose," I say.

"Then I'll start with the good. Looks like you two will get the reward money for your help in the arrest and conviction of Leah's killer."

"WE GETTIN' PAID," Blade says in the same sports announcer voice. To me she adds, "I told your ass we couldn't stop working it, that if we did it out of the goodness of our hearts good things would happen, because they always do."

"That's what you said?" I ask.

"Bitch, I'm paraphrasin', but you get the point. Stop worrying about money and just do the work. Everything will be okay."

"Yeah," Pete says, "that sounds like you."

"What's the bad news?" I ask.

"Chrissy Violet's stepmother filed a missing person report," he says. "An investigation is underway. They've assigned Bob Kirkland to the case. He's good. And relentless."

Rush looks alarmed, and I can tell she's going to be a problem.

Blade takes her hand and caresses it. "You tell him if he needs help to give us a call," she says. "We specialize in missing persons."

"Just be careful," Pete says. "Kirk is very good."

"So am I," she says.

If just hearing that there's an investigation upsets Rush, what's going to happen when she actually feels the pressure from the vice when it tightens around her?

"We knew this would happen," I say. "Just have to deal with it now. What's the other bad news?"

"Lev Sokolov was killed this morning," he says.

I nod and think about it.

Rush says, "Why is that bad news? One less Russian gangster in the world is—"

"It means there's no restraint on Dimitri now," I say. "He'll be coming for us."

"Well," Blade says, "let's make sure he knows where to find us. And who knows? Maybe he's behind Chrissy Violet's disappearance and will be arrested before he can make a run on us. You just never know with these things."

"Never stops, does it?" Lexi says. "The bad guys just keep coming."

"That's true," I say, standing, "but you know what else is true. The hits. The hits keep coming. Who's ready for some more hit tunes from the lovely and talented Cindi Rush?"

Rush stands and we make our way over to the stage, grab our guitars, and start playing again.

And instead of worrying about what Chrissy Violet's investigation means for Blade, or what Dimitri's new freedom means for all of us, or what Logan is going to blackmail me to do next, or what difficulties and dangers our next case will bring, or even whether I'll go back to prison, I play and sing with everything in me. I let the music carry me away to a better place, refusing to let what might happen in the future rob me of this moment and how good things are right now.

ALSO BY MICHAEL LISTER

Sign up for Michael's newsletter by clicking here or go to www.MichaelLister.com and receive a free book.

(John Jordan Novels)

Power in the Blood

Blood of the Lamb

Flesh and Blood

(Special Introduction by Margaret Coel)

The Body and the Blood

Double Exposure

Blood Sacrifice

Rivers to Blood

Burnt Offerings

Innocent Blood

(Special Introduction by Michael Connelly)

Separation Anxiety

Blood Money

Blood Moon

Thunder Beach

Blood Cries

A Certain Retribution

Blood Oath

Blood Work

Cold Blood

Blood Betrayal

Blood Shot

Blood Ties

Blood Stone

Blood Trail

Bloodshed

Blue Blood

And the Sea Became Blood

The Blood-Dimmed Tide

Blood and Sand

Blood Lure

Blood Pathogen

Beneath a Blood-Red Sky

Out for Blood

What Child is This?

(Jimmy "Soldier" Riley Novels)

The Big Goodbye

The Big Beyond

The Big Hello

The Big Bout

The Big Blast

In a Spider's Web (short story)

The Big Book of Noir

(Merrick McKnight / Reggie Summers Novels)

Thunder Beach

A Certain Retribution

Blood Oath

Blood Shot

(Remington James Novels)

Double Exposure

(includes intro by Michael Connelly)

Separation Anxiety

Blood Shot

(Sam Michaels / Daniel Davis Novels)

Burnt Offerings

Blood Oath

Cold Blood

Blood Shot

(Love Stories)

Carrie's Gift

(Short Story Collections)

North Florida Noir

Florida Heat Wave

Delta Blues

Another Quiet Night in Desperation